THE SACRIFICE OF ANTON STACEY

Copyright © 2020 Christian Francis.
All Rights Reserved.

The characters and events in this book are fictitious. Any similarity to real persons, living or dead is coincidental and not intended by the author.

No part of this book may be reproduced in any form or by any electronic or mechanical means, including information storage and retrieval systems, without permission in writing from the publisher, except by a reviewer who may quote brief passages in a review.

ECHO ON
PUBLISHING

Always for you Vicky xxx
- CF

CONTENTS

1. Going Home — 1
2. Cashing in the Chit — 16
3. The Old Homestead — 29
4. Goodbye, Appalachia — 45
5. The Eye's Deathly Lights — 58
6. These Rotten Streets — 74
7. The Ascension of Anton Stacey — 81
8. The Epilogue of Folksville — 88

1

GOING HOME

The Stacey brothers, in their youth, were closer than most kin were. During their formative years, they had not only grown up together and shared every waking moment in each other's company. They even shared the same bedroom until their late teens. Chosen to be homeschooled by their Father, Pastor Henry Stacey. They were taught with a religious fervor greater than even the most evangelical of the cable access television preachers; Preachers whom Henry said *Didn't go far enough!* and were *the Devil's concubines*. Pastor Henry Stacey was an incredibly pious man, who saw the fire and brimstone style of the God of the Old Testament as the true and only deity in the heavens. The New Testament was, according to his ignorance and unabashed hatred, *written by sodomites and communists*. His violent God was the one true God that ruled the household, and he lay down these teachings to his Children with an unloving and fearsome threat of Biblical wraith. It was because of this that the Stacey brothers, whom despite making a childhood pact to never leave each other's side, had not spoken to each other, in person, for decades.

Living in a large old cabin on the side of the Appalachian Mountains, the Stacey family lived a semi self-sufficient lifestyle. A stream ran behind their cabin, where sat a water generator, which gave them electricity most of the year round, that is, until the snow hit, and the freeze imprisoned the stream for months at a time , sending the cabin into the cold darkness where the Stacey's had to rely on fires to keep them warm and give them any light. There was no television here, no refrigeration, no mod-cons at all , Just walls, a fireplace, occasional electricity and the surrounding nature. This was the way the Pastor wanted it. The way God intended it.

At the bottom of the mountain was the village of Folksville; A small mining community of just over a thousand people. A God-fearing and backward community that the Pastor led from his small church, which sat on the edge of town. A church where each Wednesday and Sunday he would preach about the evils in the world , of which he thought there were plenty. Words tinged with ignorant hate spoken with passion to the rapturous applause and adulation of his flock.

Henry Stacey's teachings not only made a lasting impression on the people of Folksville, but also on the young Jacob Stacey, the oldest of the brothers. His father's words rang true in his mind and made sense of the world that he saw around him. The hatred in humanity could only be cured by adhering to his God's word. No ifs, no buts, no exceptions. *The Lord's word was written in the very stone of the earth beneath you. Yet the foolish think they can break the earth with their own hands.* This was Jacob's favorite saying of his father's and one repeated often when he himself became the Pastor of the Folksville church. But unlike his father, he had more care for the sinners. He had more love than his father was ever capable of. He had no intention of taking over the mantel of Pastor, but after his father was forced into retirement by a catastrophic stroke, he felt he had been called to action by God himself. This stroke was one which left Henry Stacey in a permanent vegetative state, and was the trigger that convinced the youngest brother, Anton, to make his escape far from his father's cruelty incapacitated or not.

On his 18th birthday, Anton had confided in his brother about something he had come to accept in himself , Something his father had referred to in other people as *abhorrent and grotesque*. But he made a mistake by wrongly thinking that his brother, his closest friend and confidant, would keep the secret safe.

"It ain't mine to hold for ya, little brother," Jacob had told him with a cold matter-of-fact demeanor. "This is for God to know, and the Pastor will help you. You have to trust in him and God."

Since both of them could remember, their father had been referred to as *the Pastor*. Not Dad, Father, Pops, or any other affectations. Without any female hand in them being raised, they were only taught by their father and he demanded they treat him as God's one disciple. He was not there to love them, but only to teach them the one truth about his God, no matter how hateful and damning.

Despite Anton's pleas, Jacob told his father of what had been confided in him. Upon hearing those words, a fury built up from within Henry, the likes of which the brothers had never seen before. Sure they had seen him angry, but this was a terrifying fury. Expecting some words of guidance, Jacob burst into tears as his father instead bellowed anger, slamming his hands down on his large oak desk, screaming about how *Satan dared turned my son into a follower of Sodom!*

He then decreed that Anton was no longer his son and that he could not allow evil into his home, one second more. So, he grabbed his youngest by the throat , intending to throw him outside. But instead, he started to choke the very life out of his small body. Though an adult by this age, Anton was barely over 5-foot-tall and stick thin, the polar opposite of his huge father, whose bear-like hands clasped around his throat like a vise , Suffocating him.

Screaming for them to stop, Jacob sobbed for clemency for his brother, but his screams were met with his Father backhanding his eldest with all of his might. Sending him reeling backwards, crashing into the wall behind.

"Don't beg for this devil!" were the last words he said before the rage within him caused an irreparable hemorrhage in his brain, ending his reign of terror forever.

The boys, keeping the events of that evening to themselves, were told by the doctors that the Pastor's stroke was of such severity that he would never recover, but he would not die; Unable to talk, unable to move and in need of constant care.

The very next day, Anton left the homestead where he grew up, abandoning the brother whom he was once so close to, far behind. Leaving him alone to care for their father. With no intention to ever return, he got on the bus and left to live his life far from the hate of the mountain. That was until he received a letter, 32 years after leaving his childhood home. A letter that told him that his father, the Pastor, had finally left his mortal coil.

Every month since he left the mountain, Anton had written letters to his brother, telling him of where he was and what he was doing, and Jacob replied just as often. Both, though separated, needed to keep a connection to each other. Their letters never mentioned that fateful night and never mentioned Jacob being left alone as caregiver. But full of doubt and reflection, Jacob always shared his innermost thoughts when he replied; Thoughts of how he would sometimes stay awake, drowning out their father's unconscious moans with a bottle of whisky. The alcohol providing a temporary relief from the only thing the Pastor did; moan loudly upon each exhalation.

"They are not cries of pain," the local doctor said to Jacob, "so rest your worry at that. He's for all intents and purposes, brain-dead. Now I don't mean that in a callous way, but we have to face what he is. These noises. They'll just happen sometimes. Think of them like snoring whilst awake." These words did nothing to quell Jacob's nightly torment, not that he trusted his doctor's diagnosis, as he seemed to be more in tune with superstitions than any real science. But there was nothing he could do about it. He just had to accept this reality he lived in.

Jacob spent his days in two guises, the first as the Pastor, planning and delivering sermons in the church at the bottom of the mountain. The second was as nurse to the now motionless body of what was his father, yet now was just a vacant slab of meat, dressed in yellowing pajamas. A slab that stared up at the same piece of ceiling every day, moaning on each breath. Unable to move, talk or even think. Just living in a hell of mindless existence. Breathing and blinking out of reflex alone. Jacob thanked his Lord for the small mercies he was given. He did not have to worry about feeding his father, as he was given sustenance intravenously. So all he had to do was change the waste bags, bathe him every other day, exercise his legs to stave off atrophy, not that it would help, and keep him presentable with a shave and brushing of his hair.

Jacob took care of his father as if he was aware of his surroundings or heard the words he spoke as he cared for him. In case he may regain his mind by some miracle, which was never to happen. Even if his version of God existed, Henry was too much of a terrible human to reward with saving.

Each day, Jacob dutifully fulfilled his caregiving role, all whilst engaging in one sided banal conversations. Then at night, he would read a sermon by his father's bedside as if reading a bedtime story to a child. Soon after turning off the light to his father's bedroom, Jacob would drink the torment away, numbing any oncoming feeling of desperation.

This was his life.

Year in year out, with no change.

No change until that slab in the bed succumbed to the darkness for good.

In the letters to his brother, Jacob tried to keep as much sadness out as possible. He tried to keep his own feelings of abandonment far away. There was no use in laying blame or resentment. He knew why Anton left, he accepted that, though he wished it had been different. Instead, he wrote about life, about his regret of not finding love. His occasional doubt about his chosen holy path in life. He wrote about wanting to one day travel, escaping the mountains he felt shackled to his entire life.

Pastor Henry Stacey. Once a larger than life man. Filled with the insurmountable fury of his faith, had been long reduce to nothing. He had been a cruel man with no love to give those who needed it most, and ended up reduced to a vacant body on a bed. For over thirty years he existed as nothing but a burden to his eldest son. Now, with the last of his life finally extinguished from his useless body, he only left a cold sack of flesh and bone.

At the moment he had noticed that his father had died, Jacob dropped to his knees. The tears that initially flooded from his eyes, soon transformed into a laugh. The crying had not come out of sadness or shock, but out of simple relief. Relief that the moaning from that living corpse that dwelled in the cabin was now forever gone. Relief that his hands would no longer carry a stench of filth after having to clean the worst places of his father. Relief that he was, at long last, *free*. His feeling of duty was now over. He had taken the burden of his father's care solely on his own shoulders, as it was something he felt his God would demand. But now, it was *over*. As the winter freeze gripped the mountain, he felt warmth inside for the first time. Warmth he felt guilty for. He was so happy his father was now dead, it filled him with equal shame.

Before Henry's body had even been picked up by the coroner, Jacob wrote a final letter to his brother. It was not the usual long and personal missive that he would normally pen , Instead it was short and simple;

My dearest Anton,

It has finally happened. I need to call in my chit (if you remember what that is). Can you come home for Saturday 14th for the burial?

Your brother,

Jacob.

In his heart, Jacob knew that Anton would not want to come home for any reason. The hadn't seen each other in person, nor heard each other's voices in over three decades. No contact was had except for what they wrote in their correspondence. Jacob *did* know what Anton looked like though, as he had followed his career as close as he could. Seeing his rise to fame from the mountain.

Marion Colt had been the librarian of Folksville for the past forty years. She had seen the world pass as the seasons rotated, through the large windows at the front of this modest library. Though a library in name, it was a lot more to the people of the town, it had to be. A town with so few residents would not be able to sustain such a place, but this town library was also the school for the few dozen children growing up here. It was Marion who taught them all from a very young age, that is until they got to high school level, when they went across the street to the larger and more equipped classrooms, to be taught by the actual teachers , Not that any of her students would ever think of her as anything less than a real teacher. They adored her. The whole town adored her, as did Jacob. He held an unrequited love for her. If times had been different, he would have chosen to court her, marry her, and maybe even start a family with her, But God's word was his life now and no matter how much he wanted, his calling had to take priority. And like Marion, he too was not officially qualified for his role. He was Pastor due to want, not due to reward , The town accepted this without question. He never had time for seminary school, and learned all the town needed him for from the words in the holy book.

The shame of the relationship between Jacob and Marion was that was she felt the same as him. She adored him despite being already married. Betrothed to a man she had felt barely a twinge of affection for, a twinge that was a small shadow compared to the sheer adoration she held for Pastor Henry's son. She could never think of Jacob as the *Pastor*, that was his father's role. Jacob was the handsome boy who used to walk with her from the sermons. Keeping her company to make sure she got home safe. It was because of this still present affection for him, that she helped him out, and kept track of Anton. With the only computers in town and the only links to the internet, the library was the perfect way to ensure that she and Jacob kept seeing each other outside of the church, away from prying eyes.

Each Monday, Jacob would come into the library to see the latest of what his brother was up to. The latest news articles. The latest scandals. Anything. He and Marion lived vicariously through the tabloid tales of his musician brother. She would spend the week searching news sites, gossip columns, social media accounts, anything at all. Then she would print all that she found and wait for Monday to come. 1pm. On the dot. After the morning class had finished. He was never late. Then, they would then sit for an hour or two, in the quiet of the reading room, far at the back of the library. They would read each other the news of the Stacey brother who succeeded in this cruel and unforgiving world.

Sitting in his dressing room, Anton counted down the hours before he had to go on stage and entertain a baying audience. His life had become somewhat of a monotony, but was one that he embraced. The limelight that he basked in for the best part of twenty years was a comforting glow. To some it was blinding and corrupting, but to him it was a shroud. Gone were the insane beginnings of his fame, with the wasting of all his earnings on drugs and lavish parties. Nowadays he would just invest his extra income and prefer to spend evenings at home with his husband , That was until the husband's wandering cock earned him a one-way ticket to an enforced prenuptial agreement. One which left this husband with nothing to show for the past 16 months of their whirlwind romance.

Soon after their divorce, Anton found himself alone in his house, deep in the Hollywood Hills. Trapped in the cage too large to be called a home. His isolation cast him back to the day he stared at his collapsed father on the floor of the cabin. Despite his brother being there, he felt alone and like he had to escape that prison. Now many years later on a different hill, he was *still* in a prison, but one of his own making , a safer prison than the cabin and one that, despite all of the restrictions, was *his* home. A place he could live how he wanted and do what he wanted. A place he could be who he wanted to be.

To escape the comfortable confinement, and to get away from the monotony of his life, he decided to embark on a year-long, worldwide tour. He didn't need the money. What he *did* need were the distractions which came with such commitments.

He had been exceptionally lucky in his journey from the mountain to Los Angeles. Taking any job that he could, no matter how menial or low paying it was, he managed to earn enough money to travel the 2,300 miles across the country. It was within a week of being in Los Angeles, that he found an after-hours job, cleaning a small music venue. A venue where at the end of each and every night, steam rose from the vomit and shit-caked toilets, creating an invisible fog which stung the eyes and contracted the lungs. It was low paid employment that few could handle for very long, but Anton didn't have any problems with it. He was cleaning up waste. Just as he had to when he was ordered to clean out the shed, the shed where his father had just butchered animals for their meat. At least here, the job paid just enough for him to afford rent on a cupboard sized apartment in skid row , A place which the owner had generously called an professional studio apartment.

Initially, he never intended to come to Los Angeles. He just wanted to go far away , As far as he could without a passport. LA was as west as he could go and was where fate led him to. Where he would find his place.

Despite being forbidden by the Pastor to play any music, Anton had always loved it. "The devil's tunes will corrupt your soul!" the Pastor would say, but thankfully, not everyone in this town shared his viewpoint; the Carson residence the other side of the Folksville had a small piano belonging to the only surviving member of that family; an 86-year-old woman named Agnes; The skeletal fierce-expressioned stalwart of this house. The type of person people referred to in nasty tones that she would *outlive the cockroaches*. Someone who on first glance seemed to have no joy within their lives. She was not one to partake in the town's frivolous events and would only ever be seen when at the store, going to church or taking a walk in the early morning. Despite her miserable reputation, she took a shine to young Anton. The boy who sat on the back pew at every sermon, looking so very sad and dejected.

She had taken it upon herself to be a good Christian, and help this young boy, as it was obvious his father had no care for him. Under the guise of doing some chores around her house, she spent every Saturday talking to Anton. Telling him about the wonders outside of the mountain. Telling him the amazing stories of her life. Though initially shy and uncommunicative, he eventually opened up to her. Telling her things that he never even told his brother. It wasn't long after that he asked about the piano which sat at the other side of her living room. Hidden under a

The Sacrifice of Anton Stacey

large decorative sheet gathering dust. Despite being forbidden to think about music, he asked if she could play and if she could, could she teach him? The answer was of course, yes.

It was over the next five years where they spent each day they had together, sat around this old instrument, playing the old classics from her younger days; Songs Anton fell in love with. His particular favorite being *Que Será Será*. A song they both enjoyed playing at the start of each lesson.

Agnes had always remarked about how wonderful his voice was. How much she loved to hear it. Though he did not put much stock in her words, he nevertheless sang anything she requested him to learn. He owed her for this, as their Saturday's were his most prized days; His secret, wonderful days. The days where he was not *the Stacey boy*, but just Anton.

All of this came to a stop though after Agnes passed away. After getting to her house for his regular time, he had noticed that the lights were still on, which was very unusual for her. Normally, as soon as the sun came up, the lights were turned off. Even when the light was low and details were hard to see, she discarded the electric illuminations in favor of Gods natural light. But here they were, still switched on, on this bright spring morning.

Finding her slumped over her piano, he soon realized that she had been there since the previous week. The same song sheet rested on the piano. The same cup of tea sat beside her. The same half eaten cake crumbed onto the plate which he had left there.

With a strong guilt seeping up on him, he started to weep. Believing that if he had stayed even an extra hour, if he had not gone home early, he could have been there for her. He could have saved her life, or at least kept her company within her final moments.

Before he contacted any of the authorities, and would be something he couldn't figure out, why he did, he sat down beside her corpse on the piano stool , The same place he had sat even days previously, and played for her, one last time.

It was that same fateful week, the week he would turn 18, that he would finally have the courage to do what Agnes asked of him. To be true to himself and himself alone.

If someone does not like you? To hell and damnation with them.

She knew full well of his preferences and she didn't care one bit. She had no judgement on him. He was as much a creation of her God as she was.

Are you hurting anyone? No? Then God sure as stuffings ain't gonna give two hoots.

Despite his coming out leading to a terrible conclusion for his familial ties, as well as the life of his father, he would never have changed what happened. It was a necessary path that led him away to another city, to a place where he would walk onto the stage , in the venue where he cleaned up the piss and the shit – under the banner of Open Mic Night, and sit at the house piano and play a song.

That song.

The song he sang at every lesson.

The song he, on the first night, dedicated to Agnes.

Any other person singing such an old song in this venue, would have probably garnered little more than a smattering of polite applause , but *that* night, with *that* particular audience. Something struck a chord in the zeitgeist within those four walls. Maybe it was his voice. Maybe it was the collected emotion of the times they lived in. Maybe it was just fortune smiling down, but after a rapturous applause, he sang another. One he had never played to anyone. One he wrote as he travelled away from the mountain. One he called *Goodbye Appalachia*.

From that night of strange and amazing success, the owner

The Sacrifice of Anton Stacey

took Anton off cleaning duty, as he saw something he hadn't seen for a long time, genuine untapped talent. He was looking for a performer to take a regular slot in the venue, playing on non-gig nights to entertain any drinkers who may choose to drift in. In Anton, he saw no better person. Of course, he would be paid the same. He knew Anton would say yes, no matter what. Despite believing in his talent, the owner was a shrewd business man who held onto every penny that he could.

From this offer onwards, Anton started to write down everything he thought. These thoughts he would then put to the music of a simple piano; Anything and everything he felt. No matter how raw. No matter how painful. *Hands Around My World* being about his father trying to kill him. *Brother Man* being about him wishing he could have seen his brother grow up into the man he became. But it was always *Goodbye Appalachia* that was the song that people wanted to hear above all others. The one he wrote on the back seat of the Greyhound, the one which cleansed him of the hate he had endured on the Mountain.

It was less than 3 years later, after playing a set twice a week in that venue, that Anton was offered a recording contract. His nights playing to a few people had blossomed into a strong following, where his nights had bigger audiences than the name acts that stood on this same stage. It was only another 7 years after that, where he had his first headline concert at Madison Square Garden.

Now sat in his dressing room of the Hollywood Bowl, about to perform his last concert from his mammoth tour, he stared into the mirror reflecting on his world. This was his homecoming gig to the town that made him. It was also here where 10 minutes prior, his assistant brought him a hand-written letter. One that was sent to his home earlier that day. One which the assistant had opened, as she did all his mail and was one she had brought to him with a look of worry.

"I'm so sorry, I know you're about to go on, but I thought this was too important," she said as he took the letter.

He had always wondered what he would feel like when his father died. Amusement? Nonchalance? He did not know for sure, but he did not expect the one that hit him; Sadness. A wave of emotion hit him square in the face causing him to cry more than he had done since leaving the mountain.

That night, under the bright glare of the stage lights, as his audience stood in adulation of him, instead of singing *Que Será Será* as it was written, he changed the lyrics to the ones he had written the night he left for the bus station. Prefacing it with a tearful address to the gathered masses.

"People say I share too much in my lyrics," he said with a waver in his voice into the microphone. Though his face was hidden in the shadows, the audience knew he was crying. "So, I say fuck them. Here is something more. A bigger peek behind the curtain. I just found out that my father, my estranged abusive father, is dead."

The crowd stood in shock at this revelation. People had wondered about his father for years. There were no records anyone could find, and he always refused to address questions about it , He only ever referred to anything personal in song, and his father in vague fleeting terms.

"And my brother, Jacob. He's a Pastor in a small mountain town. He asked me to go home to bury that asshole."

Turning to the piano keys he placed his hands above them, ready to play. "And this is about why I left."

He started to play *Que Será Será* but with his rewritten lyrics;
When I was just a little boy, I asked my father, please accept me.
With his own hands, he choked me out.
And grinning he said with glee.

The Sacrifice of Anton Stacey

You're a sodomite.
And you're no son of mine.
You have to leave this place.
You're no son of mine.

Stopping after the first verse, he paused before shaking his head, apologizing and continuing to sing the song as it was originally written.

When he left the stage after the second encore, his adoring fans remained chanting for more. He got into his car and without even a thought of rest, he left Los Angeles. He ignored the pleas of his staff to not travel that distance alone, shrugging them off he began his long journey back to the mountain.

2

CASHING IN THE CHIT

This year, the big freeze had come early to Folksville. The heavy blizzards had swept through the streets with such force, that most of the town had no choice but to close. For the past month, the snow had coated the entire mountain with a thick and ghost-white powder, blocking off most access in and around Folksville.

The town was more than used to this happening, as it came at some point each year. Though the stores themselves may have been closed, though some streets were impassable, the people still went about their day, they still lived their lives as best they could. The food market doors were closed due to the street being inaccessible, but they still took orders over the phone and made deliveries on foot where needed.

The dirt track which led from the town up to the cabin was cleared daily by the local handyman, Jimmy Mons. A man who had taken it upon himself to use his snow plow to help the Pastor, a service which he usually charged people for. It was though free to the Pastor in a vain attempt by Mons to atone for his past *indiscretions*.

Surely helping a man of God would get me a pass? was his think-

The Sacrifice of Anton Stacey

ing. This was an attempt at salvation that Jacob was more than grateful for, but would never offer God's forgiveness for what that man once did. That was between him and the Lord. All he could offer was solace in his penance on his path to divine absolution.

Jacob sat in his truck. The windshield wipers weakly pushed off the snow that had settled down over the past few hours. The blizzard itself had mainly stopped its constant barrage. The only evidence left of its presence was an occasional icy downpour. But that was not to last for long. The storms above were brewing ominously, as if the Gods were angry.

His eyes were wide as he watched the snow being brushed away from his view. Then staring into his rear-view mirror, at the reflection of the back of his pick-up. He looked at the black coffin which lay there. Sat like a large negative mass against the blue rusted paint of his cargo bed, with a thick blanket of snowflakes resting on its top. Though the coffin carried the body of his father, it was not real to him, *none* of this was. He wondered to himself how was that blight which hung around his neck for decades, no longer in existence? He could never admit his disdain and hatred out loud, but he couldn't help but resent his duty to care for his father. Ever since the Pastor strangled Anton, Jacob lost all love and respect he had for that man and knowing he could not hide his feelings from his God, he carried on each day in silent resentment, hoping his true feelings would mean nothing on the day of his death. The day he would answer to his Lord. He hoped that his actions in life would counteract any and all negative thoughts he had for who was now just a decaying corpse in a coffin.

When Anton had left, Jacob had no choice but to face the full fury of the congregation alone. With them demanding to know what would happen to their church, as they mourned the loss of their leader , he had no other choice but to stand up to the podium and put to use the words of *his* faith.

It had been a hard struggle to speak these new words of compassion and forgiveness. Words that the church were at first not receptive to. In the beginning, he had made a conscious effort to change the message of the church. Though railing loudly, he didn't preach about evil, as he didn't think evil was a prominent part of humanity, a total opposite to what his father had preached. Instead, he spoke of acceptance and peace in a misleading damning tone. This lost him some members who only were there to fuel their righteous indignation and intolerances, whether wishing to hate anyone black, gay, communist, they had looked to Pastor Henry to amplify their ludicrous notions of right and wrong. But those days were gone.

For a while, Jacob only retained a small handful of followers, but as word spread and he became more active within the town itself, people started to attend. Even if they didn't truly believe. They came because they liked Jacob and his words of peace. From his running of community events such as harvest celebrations, hosting film nights, collecting for the poor, Jacob did anything he could to serve the thousand residents of Folksville. He even was Santa each year for the children. Each Saturday during the month of December, Bruce's hardware store would clear out one end of the shop, and erect a makeshift grotto. On a decorated chair within it, Jacob would sit complete with his red outfit, fake beard and fat suit. Ho-ho-ho'ing as if he actually *was* St Nick. Pastor Henry had previously deemed Santa Claus as an effigy of Satan; *The clues in the name. For the love of Mary our mother, open your eyes! He was made by the Jews and Homosexuals to corrupt your children!*

For Jacob though, as well the residents of the town who were not so hateful and ignorant, Santa was a welcome message of love to children. Something that offered them hope and goodwill, something Jacob took to heart with aplomb.

The Sacrifice of Anton Stacey

As he found himself staring at the coffin in the rear-view mirror, he forced his attention away. That man had drawn his notice for long enough.

If Anton *was* going to return, he would be there soon. The coroner did him a favour and kept the body on ice an extra week, giving him enough time to send Anton the letter, to hope his request would be met with acceptance, and his brother would return for the burial; Not that Jacob thought this was even a possibility, but he held out hope none the less. The pact they made in their treehouse was committed before adult life took over and stole his brother away. They were adults now, and a childish pact may be something Anton would put no real stock in anymore. He may not even remember what a *chit* was to them.

The treehouse was their fort growing up; their refuge. A place they had built and exhausted their younger years in. Set about half a mile from the cabin, deep within the forest, there lay a small clearing of three fallen trees. These huge giants lay across each other and created a space below them. With Anton being scared of heights, the then 7-year-old Jacob decided that they could make something of this space, so started a summer mission to build their secret hideout. Away from their father. Somewhere far from the burning eyes of the biblical Lord they were daily threatened with. A place he could never know about.

Under the guise of going to do some menial chores within the town, they went looking for any scrap wood or other materials they could use to build their new hideaway. Putting all of their haul into a red wooden hand pulled wagon, they then trekked their materials up the mountain and into the woods. Their new fort built out of anything they could find.

Even into their teens they spent many hours in their ground level den. With the three large fallen trees laying overhead making their roof, they were protected from sight, as well as from the harsher weather. From the outside, nothing could be seen except undergrowth billowing from the trees above. Jacob and Anton had built a small hidden place within this brush, as well as covered the outside walls with branches, masking its existence from prying eyes. Even the door handles they fashioned from old car doors were hidden behind the leaves.

The pact they made in this fortress was a simple one; That if the other asked, no matter what for, the other would be there. Without needing any explanation. Without needing any persuading. A pact that would be cashed in many times during the following years, when the going got too rough in the Stacey household , Jacob called this pact their chits , And each brother had them to use when something was really needed of the other. A code word to let the other one know that it was not just a simple thing that was being asked. This was invented primarily as a means for Anton to safely let Jacob know how serious things were, since Anton was the focus of persecution from the Pastor. "I gotta cash in my chit" Anton said on many occasions, either to talk or when words had left him and he just needed to cry on his brother's shoulder. It was these chits that were *always* spent in regards to their father. He was their only bully in the town. Their only fury. Their only hate. His beatings and mental abuse had always been focused on the smallest of the brothers. Jacob never quite knew why. Was it because Anton took less of an interest in the faith than the rest of the family? Or was it because his birth led to the death of their mother? He would never know, but he would always be there for Anton. No matter what. The chits would always be there *for* him.

In the last letter Jacob sent to Anton, that had been the first and only time that Jacob would ever use one of their chits. This was the reason Anton left that night to drive back to the mountain. Without a pause for thought, to Anton it was not even a question of will I? It was instead I will! He would never have come home *just* for his father's burial. But for his brother asking to cash in the chit, he had to come. It was not a small thing that this was the first time that his brother had ever asked anything of him. In all their childhood and later correspondence, Jacob never *once* asked for a thing. He gave updates on the town and talked about events he had seen in his brother's life, but never asked for him to come home, or lamented that night, or asked for money. Jacob was a proud man and would only ever ask for anything if there was no other choice.

It was also in their treehouse that Anton confessed to Jacob. The confession that started it all, which Jacob would never forgive himself for betraying. Hoping that the Pastor would accept the revelation as much as he did. He thought it would be better than living in fear that if the Pastor found out that Jacob knew and *didn't* tell him, would result in a much, *much* worse outcome for all. Jacob was devastated when he saw the rage erupt from within his father's eyes. The clenched fists. The bellowing voice. The veins popping up on his reddened face. The mistake Jacob had made that night weighed heavily on his head for many years. Though he hated his father, and believed that what happened to him was some holy payback handed down from the angels under his silent prayer , he held himself ultimately responsible for everything. So, as he *was* responsible, he had no other choice but to do all he *could* to pay this angel debt back, and live his life doing good for his father's body, addressing the angelic balance.

In his later years, he dismissed this unconstructive blame, he was only young after all. Living under the Sword of Damocles that was his father's holy wrath, would push any impressionable person to do almost any wrong. Through the power of hindsight, he could see the abuse that the Pastor laid down upon them. The beatings, the punishments, all under the guise of earning forgiveness from the Lord. At the time, it had seemed normal, but as he got older and wiser, he came to realise that his father was an evil man full of hate and ignorance. A man who not only treated his children like slaves, but beat them for even the slightest invented infraction. A man who hated almost all of the world, and claimed his God felt the same.

Each night as the Pastor lay in his vegetative state, moaning aloud with each breath, in the exhausting moments before sleep took him away, Jacob had laid in his own bed staring up to the darkness. Daydreaming of him walking into his father's room, screaming at him about all he had done wrong. Laying down the law of how his actions were evil, all before picking up a pillow and suffocating the life from his body. These daydreams never really changed in content. They were his way of trying to cope with the situation.

With Anton gone so soon after the stroke, he had nothing of a family left in this place. Sure he had the congregation and the people of the town, but no actual blood apart from the mass of meat that moaned in its braindead fugue, deep in what was their old bedroom.

Putting his father in that room, in Anton's old bed, was the best 'fuck you' Jacob could think of doing. Placing a picture of this hated son on the bedside, was the cherry on the cake. A constant reminder to any part of him that may still be present, that *he* was the one who lost. That Anton got away. That what he felt now was God's righteous punishment for an unrighteous man.

As he drove out of the snow-covered town, then onto the recently plowed dirt track up the mountain, Jacob wondered how long he should wait before burying his father. How long he should wait for Anton.

It was Saturday 14th now. Only a few hours remained of the day on which he asked Anton to come home. *He may not have even seen the letter.* Jacob mused to himself, *it may have been lost in transit, it wouldn't be the first time the postal service lost a letter, or he had a commitment that he couldn't get out of.* Even now he was making excuses for his brother not coming back, not knowing that he had arrived at the cabin an hour before. As Jacob was picking up the coffin from the funeral home, Anton was sat in his car, after slowly driving up the mountain and now looked out of his windshield. Looking at the place he had called home for the first 18 years of his life , The place of much hardship and woe.

Marion Colt thought that it would be quick.

One step into nothingness was all that it was supposed to take.

She knew it was wrong; Pastor Jacob's Father had railed against it, calling it the *miscreants escape to hell*. Pastor Jacob, though, he eschewed the teachings of forgiveness and kindness, as well as exceptions to rules. One of his sermons concerned a convicted felon who had killed his own son with an axe, though a reprehensible crime, Pastor Jacob talked about how no one person was innately evil, that their circumstance and background shaped them to do evil things, so their crime did not mean they could not be forgiven by God, as a piece of good may still dwell inside of them. And God would never punish good. So, as Marion gasped for breath and clawed at her neck, she knew that she was sorry for what she had done, but had already prayed to be forgiven only moments before.

Twenty minutes earlier she had no thought that led to this moment. She was puttering around her library, cleaning the book shelves, putting them in order, not that they were ever out of order , Only a few books were taken out each day, so they were easy for one person to manage. Nevertheless, no matter how busy or quiet the library may be over a season, Marion wanted to always maintain the building to be the cleanest and most orderly library in America.

Whilst cleaning the large window at the front of the building, overlooking the main street into town. The same window she had seen that man she deemed a monster, Johnny Mons, plowing with his truck , she had seen a car slowly drive by through the drifting snow. Driving carefully so as not to skid into the parked cars which lined the streets, carefully navigating through the parting in the deep blanket of snow. In this car, she saw a face she had seen more than most others in town. Her years spent following him online , Collating information for her beloved Jacob. A face she had not seen since in person since he was a young man, that of Anton Stacey.

Her heart sank as she saw him drive past the library, glancing out at the town he once knew. As his eyes met hers, he instinctively smiled at her. Her reaction back was one of pure shock, with no ability to return the expression.

She *knew* what his coming home meant. She had been allowed by Jacob to see any and all correspondence the brothers had shared. In one of them, she remembered Anton wrote that when Jacob was free from their father, he would like to bring him to Los Angeles. He could be the one person that Anton could trust in that town of fakery and lies. A person Anton sorely needed. Though Jacob would never admit it, she could tell that it was what he truly wanted. So, now with Pastor Henry dead, and Jacob free, Anton was here to take away the only person she loved, even if it was a silent love.

Without much of a thought of anything more, she had seen her hope die in the form of the youngest Stacey brother arriving. She fashioned a noose from rope at the base of the outside flagpole. A flagpole which was being refreshed with a brand-new flag to replace the moth eaten one that had hung there for nearly sixty years. With the flag arriving as soon as the snowfall would let up, it would have given the library a much-needed look of renewal. Now though, that was to not happen. Not with this rope anyway.

Stepping off from the main library desk, she did not consider how others may discover her. In the middle of this large room, looming over everything like a grotesque centerpiece, she would hang by her neck as if on display for a higher purpose than her own escape from the inevitable.

Thinking the darkness would come at her like a freight train was something she had hoped for and something she had seen in her youth. Having witnessed her mother escape life in the same way, she had the experience that it was a quick and easy way, but unlike her mother's escape from her life, Marion's neck did not snap. There was no instant darkness.

Suffocating on the tightening rope, Marion's bowel and bladder had started to give way, escape her underwear and dripped down her legs, onto the newly buffed floorboards below.

She felt the liquid pool out of her tear ducts and as her vision reddened, she realised that it was blood that was dripping out. As the air was slowly stolen from her, the bloody tears dripped down and off her chin.

The shame and embarrassment of how she would be found was now at the forefront of her mind. It was a greater pain to her than the pain of her approaching end.

As she had soiled herself, the stench of her insides started to fog up the room. She could not smell anything at that moment, though, as she was too frantic in trying to tear off the rope with her hands, yet she could somehow sense it was there. She felt utter horror and indignity as she grappled with the thick old rope that crushed her throat. She scrambled to get free and prayed to every God to save her, but none came as her body jerked. With this convulsion, her hands contracted, ripping two fingernails off against the rope as they did.

And with that last pain, Marion was gone.

Before stepping onto the desk, her spoken aloud prayers for a quick release and forgiveness, were mostly mumbled and half-hearted. Yet as the life faded away out of her, with the noose tightening more with each second, her pleas for her Lord to save and forgive her were screamed silently within in her mind , and these were the prayers that were deafening and heartfelt.

And so, Marion Colt, the Librarian of Folksville, dangled from the rope by her crushed windpipe. Her body still swayed from the commotion of her final moments, as her waste dripped down onto the floor below.

Despite these final minutes of anguish, Marion went out on her *own* terms, little did she know, that she was one of the lucky ones. As life escaped her twitching body, her desperate shameful death was a peaceful, sublime escape compared to the events that would soon befall the denizens of this town.

Anton was standing on the wooden porch of the cabin, looking into its window, which had been frosted over from the cold. The ice was too thick to see much apart from the outlines of some of the darkness inside.

He presumed it would look the same as it did when he had left. Maybe a foolish thought, especially with Jacob in charge. Yet, seeing a fuse box on the porch wall, as well as a phone line coming down from the rooftop and trailing its way through the air and into the town, had caught him by surprise. Of course, his brother would get electricity and a phone. After the isolation and harsh winters of their youth, he would not have willingly stayed in that torment, not with the option to be warm and connected. Yet still, Anton was somehow taken aback by it.

Looking up at the doorframe, he wondered if there was still a key resting on top, hidden from sight, as everyone seemed to do in that area if they locked their door at all. But, to his surprise, there was nothing. No key. Times *had* changed. He didn't know if he was happy about that or sad that he missed it.

Of course times had changed. Many years had gone by without him here. Many seasons come and gone. He looked around and realised he knew nothing of this place any more. Nothing apart from what it used to be. His memory of this area was not the best, as all he remembered was his father's abuse and his brother's love , so at that moment, he started to feel slightly worried. He did not actually know his brother anymore. He had not seen him for longer than they had lived together for. Sure he had the letters from him, but they were just that. They never really showed the totality of the man Jacob had become. Hell, he could be a stone-cold bastard like his father for all Aston knew.

Jacob's eye lit up as he turned off the engine to his Pickup truck. Looking with joy at the top-of-the-line Tesla, which Anton had parked outside of the cabin.

His grin stretched further than it had done for years as he saw his little brother, looking exactly as he had seen him in the many pictures online. So much so, he had a feeling like he knew this grown man well, though in reality it was only through the media's glaring eye.

Getting out of his truck he took off his thick rimmed Stetson and smiled. "The wanderer returns!" he said aloud and with a happy tone.

Anton noticed his brother's face , The many lines that now appeared as age had crept over him. Though only in his early 50s, his face had been weathered and beaten by the harsh climate, as well as the years of struggling to maintain his composure with what life had dealt him.

He felt a pang of sadness seeing this old man with a slight paunch walk up to him. This man now a ghost of that young, strong, good looking brother that he used to admire so much. Though only a few years younger, Anton looked in his 30s, bar a few greying hairs, and only had a couple of laugh lines. The years of living in LA and the great doctors which he could afford, obviously gave him a distinct advantage. Being in the limelight he had an expectation to maintain a healthy lifestyle. So ate well, exercised, adopted a skincare regime. He was looking the best he possibly could, as opposed to Jacob who looked as worn and as beaten as the Stetson he held in his hand.

Hiding his sadness at his brother's appearance, he returned the smile. "Where's the music?" he said. "The streamers? The parade? This ain't a homecoming!"

"Well," Jacob said as he got close to his brother. "You're here now. I'm sure I can find a party hat, and some balloons somewhere in the cabin."

Smiling, they hugged each other tightly, three decades late. They both tried their best to keep composure and maintain some joviality, but quickly they lost control as the pent-up sadness they both felt from missing each other swept over them like a tidal wave.

Anton had no idea if he even *should* cry now.

He had only felt tears on his cheeks once since he was a young boy , When he read that letter.

Other than that, he had not cried once since the bus first brought him to LA. Of course, he had felt sadness. He had felt loss; When his cat died. When his husband cheated. But somehow, he had never cried.

Yet here he stood, sobbing into the arms of a man who was once the closest friend he could and would ever have.

3

THE OLD HOMESTEAD

Opening the door to the cabin, Anton thought he would smell that once familiar, now long forgotten odor that his childhood home carried when he lived here. But after thirty years, nothing felt familiar anymore. Sure, there were objects he thought that he recognized; the sofa, a couple of side boards, the huge mounted deer head on the wall (which he had always been terrified of) but all of the objects felt foreign. As if someone had seen his old home and tried to recreate it from a bad memory, it really could have been anyone's cabin.

The electricity that had been fitted throughout the cabin, now fed the three matching lamps which were placed at various parts in the room, each casting a welcoming orange glow across the dark brown hue of the furniture/ It filled all the old shadows with it's warm illumination.

Anton glanced back to his brother who had shut the door, and was now hanging his black Stetson on a coat stand.

"You drive *all* that way?" Jacob asked, taking off his jacket and putting it on a hook alongside his hat.

"Yeah, wasn't too bad. Stopped in Albuquerque and Oklahoma, so it was, well, it was Albuquerque and Oklahoma, so wasn't too exciting," Anton replied as he followed suit, taking off his coat, standing in the room awkwardly, not knowing where to go or what to do with it. Should he hang the coat himself? Should he sit down with it? Or wait to be asked? He had no idea so decided to play it safe and let his brother, now master of this cabin, offer up any guidance. He continued, "It was smooth sailing till I hit Damascus on the 58. Then, *boy* the weather took a turn."

Jacob grinned as he walked over to Anton and took his coat. "The freeze this year has been a doozy. Took us all off-guard two months earlier than expected." Walking back to the coat rack he hung his brother's coat over his. "Only just started to let up in the last few days, well, since-" stopping he had realised that the blizzard had started to clear once his father had died. "Wow, I guess since he went, but its back now from the looks of the sky."

"You know what happened to Wysteria?" Anton enquired.

"The lake?" Jacob asked curiously. "What about it?"

"I drove by it," Anton shrugged. "Well, where it used to be. It's just gone."

Jacob's confusion remained "Used to be? What d'you mean?"

"Just a big hole in the ground now. Water's nowhere to be seen," Anton said as he glanced toward his brother, still unable to shake the sorrowful feeling of how much of this man's life he had missed. This man who now carried such a sadness in his eyes. A sadness that he did not have as a child. A sadness that did not seem evident in the many letters they had written to each other over the years.

"I would've heard if that place dried up. But, you never know. Can't see how it could, though. I mean, it's a lot of water. Maybe your eyes are playing tricks on you?"

"I can only say I saw what I saw," Anton replied as he watched his brother turn around and glance out of the frosted window.

"Oh, I'm not callin' you a liar, little brother, just not something

I've heard about. But, gotta say, stranger things have happened. God sure makes it difficult for us to maintain a reality nowadays."

Jacob stared out toward the bed of his pick-up truck, to where their father's coffin now lay. Noticing where his brother was staring, Anton changed the subject "He'll be ok there tonight, right?" he asked.

Jacob nodded as he turned back around "Sure." He then motioned for his brother to take a seat on the sofa. "Don't stand on ceremony, little brother. This place is as much as yours as mine."

"It's yours all the way," Anton said as he smiled and sat down on the sofa. The same solid sofa that he hated so much as a youth, but with a dull pain now embracing his spine, caused by his long cross-country drive, the sofa's overly firm support was welcome. "You've done well with it. Finally got some light and heat in here."

"If that man thought I'd spend another moment in an icebox, he had another thing coming. But apart from that, not much else changed round here. Bedrooms are kinda the same," Jacob grinned, as he continued, "which reminds me. You gonna be okay on the sofa?"

"To sleep? Sure. Why?" Anton asked. "Bedroom out of action?"

"I think you'd prefer it here. Your bed," Jacob started, as he shrugged apologetically "well, it kinda became the Pastor's."

"Oooof!" Anton laughed, "He must have *hated* that!"

Jacob smiled and walked over toward the kitchen, all whilst keeping his attention on Anton. "Nothing less than the old bastard deserved," he said. "Anyway, enough of this dwelling on that man. We can do enough of that tomorrow when we take him up top."

"Fair enough."

"I think it's finally time we drink the forbidden bottle."

Anton looked confused, but as he thought about the phrase 'forbidden bottle', his memories blossomed in his thoughts as if from nowhere, showing him the images from his youth. The Pastor never allowed alcohol in the house. He never even allowed communion wine at his services, citing it all as the *devil's heathen piss infecting the sanctity of piousness*. No matter what anyone read out from the bible stating the opposite, he would always reply, *I don't follow that version of events* , Referring to the New Testament. *Written by corrupt devil worshipers,* was the Pastor's other colourful phrase about that book, and was one memory which Anton now thought of. Despite all of that piousness, the Pastor kept *one* bottle; A bottle of cognac that his father had given him to keep, one that he allowed in his house only as a symbol. A symbol of obedience to teach his own children. The lesson that they should honour their father's wishes even if they didn't like what was being asked. After all, he himself kept a bottle of alcohol on the shelf above the fireplace, despite not drinking and citing liquor as evil and against God, he said "*If I can do that for my father, you have no excuse in doing what I ask you.*"

Reaching up, Jacob picked the dust-caked bottle from the mantle. The label was now so worn, the text on the yellowing paper was now barely readable.

"Wow, I'd forgotten all about that," Anton said as he watched his brother blow a huge amount of dust from off of the bottle.

Smirking as the dirt particles drifted to the floor, revealing more of the dark liquid within, Jacob spoke softly as he reflected on the memory, getting slightly maudlin at his realization. "Weird how I clean this place so often, but never this. Never even touched it. Never even noticed it."

"The fear of the Pastor lives on, I guess," Anton muttered whilst glancing around at the room. Jacob obviously cleaned this place thoroughly and often , doing so as regularly as when he was a child. Carrying on his chores long after their father could order it.

"Well, no longer," Jacob said, snapping himself out of his thoughts and holding the bottle up toward his brother, "tonight, we raise a glass to something long overdue."

"Only a glass?" Anton joked with a smile.

Jacob returned the smile and corrected himself. "Okay fine, we raise a *bottle* to something long overdue."

Neither of the Stacey brothers had doubted or second guessed, for even a solitary moment, that their father's wishes for his body after death would not be carried out. They had been commanded on many occasions to obey what he wanted done after he ascended to his God's side. Almost as if he knew how his children felt about him and wanted to make sure they didn't just throw his corpse into the trash bins, round the back of the food market.

His request was simple enough in words. Take him to the top of the mountain and bury him on Echo's Point , There the Lord would welcome him. On the few occasions that he went up the mountain with his children, he would show them exactly where he wanted to rest. Echo's Point was not on any maps, but was a piece of land that flattened out near the lowest peak of the mountain above them, which he had chosen to name himself.

As children, they would privately joke about their father's burial, and talk about in whispers how they would sit him in a chair up there, a bottle of booze in his hand, with a book on communism in the other. All whilst wearing a *black power* t-shirt and no pants, it was a subject of much amusement that neither of them had forgotten. Yet now, they would fulfil his wish to the letter. Anton, despite hating the Pastor with every fibre in his being, would still help his brother in honouring the dead man's wishes. He hadn't planned to. But the chit had been called in. So there was no argument.

Normally a government would not allow for a dead body to be taken and buried by a family outside of designated burial sites, but in the case of the police of Folksville, they had their own way of doing things. They saw beyond the nation's law, and they thought that if a body has been cleared by the coroner and that all costs were met then a family; they could take the body and bury it at an agreed place. As long as the area of burial was approved, only two rules had to be followed; The hole had to be no less than 4 feet deep and the body had to be buried in the coffin. The cemetery itself was only a tiny fraction of the size it normally should be, for a population like was in Folksville.EWspecially for a town which had settled here so long ago.

The Pastor, as with many others in the town, had reserved a particular resting place on the mountain. So much so that the council kept a map, the Dead Map, which was a guide to all known burial sites in the town and its surrounding areas. He did not have to call in any special favours or pay money for this, as he was given this reservation gratis (unlike the other citizens who would need to pay if they wanted to be buried outside of the graveyard). Though the Pastor was a large, imposing and important man, it was his standing as a holy man which gave him this benefit of a free reservation.

The Dead Map itself pre-existed the Folksville police force and council, and was a tradition dating back to when the first pilgrims settled here. When those people first saw the beauty of the land, they wished to become part of it forever, not wanting to be confined to a small dark corner of a solemn cemetery , with all the corpses huddled together in their death , They wanted to be one with the land, and that is the way it always had been.

Of course, there were many who did not pay the cost to be part of this map, who were left with the cheaper option of being interred in the overgrown and badly maintained Folksville cemetery. The town cared so little for this area, that once you were buried in its dirt, with your headstone erected, that was it. On the Appalachian's behind the town, though, it was a different story.

The Sacrifice of Anton Stacey

There were small white markers at various places over the mountain. Each marker was adorned with, simply, a name and bible verse. Hundreds of them decorated the land and had become part of a regular pilgrimage by the townsfolk. On walks they would cross themselves in respect past any marker. More than they did when they passed the cemetery.

Up on the invented Echo's Point, there were no markers yet and was the reason the Pastor deemed this his *chosen* place. He had made sure that no one else was in his clearing, by blocking the whole area out on the Dead Map. This was not a large area in the context of the map itself, it was just enough to afford him a forever solitude. The death map was huge and detailed the entire area, the whole way around the three sides of the town, and over to the other side of the mountain. The Pastor's area was just a small mark on an expansive landscape , A landscape littered with hundreds of other buried bodies from the past centuries. The Pastor though, wanted solace in his rest, not companionship.

Echo's Point was not always empty, though , There had been a body there before. Marked on the map in pencil many years ago, along with a name; 'Morris Kasovic'. A name which the Pastor had hidden by writing his own in pen over the fading pencil. A devious move which no one was any the wiser of.

The Pastor would not allow anyone else up there with him. Not even his children. No one. Especially one with a *commie surname*. Which was the justification he gave himself for getting his children to dig up the area of land beneath Morris' marker. With a view of the whole town and beyond stretching out before them, Anton and Jacob broke the earth with their shovels on that summer morning, and dug for hours until they reached an old wooden casket.

They were both told that this body had to be moved, as it was buried here by mistake, neither boy knew that his father just took the coffin away and threw it into Wysteria lake which lay to the east of the town. As he cracked open the coffin lid, the Pastor emptied the cloth and bones which lay within, off from the jetty and down into the watery depths, then dropped the broken coffin wood in after them. In later years, a bone or two would wash ashore, but people would presume them to be bear bones, or some other wild animal's remains. No one would ever know, that it was a discarded corpse of Morris Kasovic. The one-time saloon owner in the new settler's town of Folksville.

Outside, the midnight freeze draped over the township, after leaving them to a few days of respite, and the dreams that the blizzards had abated for that year. But the winter was far from over. Throughout the day, the new flurry of snowflakes had started to fall. The hope that the cold had now passed until the next seasons rotation was now quashed. As fast as the day's sunlight had dissipated from the mountain, the darkness now crept in with glee. Bringing with it a haunting, howling wind to match its increasingly heavier falling of snow. A falling attack to once more recoat the vista with its thick ice-cold blanket.

Elsewhere in the town, something sinister was about to happen.
Something dark and violent.
As Marion Colt, whose body was still undiscovered , hung motionless from the library ceiling. Dangling with her throat crushed and the floor beneath her coated with dried excrement, a creeping horror went from house to house; An invisible odourless force.

No one knew what had happened. Nothing was on the television, nor on the radio. No panic had been raised. No alarm bells rang out. The blizzard outside shielded all of the people from real-

The Sacrifice of Anton Stacey

izing what they were about to share. No one rushed outside to get help in this snow storm, as no one had the time.

Each family was, this night, knowingly trapped in their own homes , fully aware of the brutal and raging weather system outside that made the streets impassable and impossible to navigate. Knowing that they could not leave. Unknowing of the brutal and raging fates which made its way closer to them. The snow was now so thickly falling, that the darkness which the night brought in was blocked out by the brightness of the midnight snow reflecting the street lights.

What they did not know was that not only *could* they not leave, but they *would* never leave their homes again.

As each person stayed in their home, watching their evenings program, or drinking their loneliness into a forced slumber , one by one this presence started to visit them.

House by house, like a wave washing through each doorway, every single person started their end by feeling an element of nausea. Initially a fleeting feeling, yet soon giving way to a thumping headache. A headache which quickly built and built to a colossal migraine, and far beyond that.

Though some people at first could manage the pain they carried in their heads, others were debilitated at the first sign of the illnesses appearance. Indiscriminately it hit both children and the aged together, the head pain caused them all to cry out from the hideous pressure within them. A cry which was masked by the stormy howls from the sky.

If they had stood outside, they may have seen what travelled through each street. Crawled its way through the snow as their pain had reached its apex. Beyond the protective sheets of thick snowflakes, slithering on the powder covered asphalt, a dark rot crept. Streaking its way with tendril-like growths. Spilling out from its path and staining the white ground into a deep and liquid-black. Like a rotting mold growing over a fallen apple, but at incredibly increased speed, this dark matter cracked and grew through the fallen snow, as it spread down the center of every street, through Folksville and toward the direction of the mountain. Travelling unseen by any eyes, it crawled silently as it worked its way within the snow that fell, growing larger and larger as it took its path down each street, and one by one spread out from the ground, leaving its black markings in the snow it had stained; from its path on the streets, it spread out and crawled over cars, mailboxes, street signs, and every building it came across.

Inside the homes, the people's cries of pain grew to a deafening din, silenced on the outside by the raging wind which howled like a banshee. The storm blew the top layers of snow to places it may never have reached normally, which gave this rot additional paths to take. Better access to its victims.

Fergus Gillan, an expatriated Irishman, had come to Folksville in his late teens from the emerald isle. Falling in love with the town, he never left. Never followed his dream of travelling the nation. In the decades he had lived here, he had seen the town flourish from a small backwoods pocket of America, to a slice of Norman Rockwell perfection. With three marriages failed and in the dust far behind him, he had now, finally, found the love of his life. *The* one. The one he was always *meant* to find. On his 75th birthday, as he sat in the town hall listening to the police chief prattle on about the new parking zones needing to come into force, he saw her. He saw Betty; A couple of years his junior, sitting at a table at the far end of the room, pouring a cup of tea for herself. A cup of what Betty charmingly referred to as 'town hall hot piss'. Never a woman to ever be called demure, Betty was foul-mouthed but a kind-hearted woman. She had only just moved to the town that year. With no family to speak of, she decided to uproot from Denton, Ohio to come to the town she had visited as a child. The town where her grandparents had come from, and a place where she felt a pull to come and settle in.

After an initial awkward exchange in the aftermath of that banal town meeting, Betty and Fergus hit it off. Though in the twilight of their years, they felt like teenagers as they soon fell into an almost constant state of copulation; every day, many times, it barely let up except for food, sleep or hospital visits. For the first few weeks, they only bothered getting clothed to go outside, as these two aged lovebirds made love as often as they could, without any care in the world.

Now both octogenarians, nothing much had changed or subsided. Their age had not slowed them down at all.

On this dark night, the effect from the black rot outside was to hit their house before anyone else's. Being the first house on the outside of town, theirs was the initial homestead that everyone would pass, on what was the only street into town; This house signalled the start of Folksville to many locals. A house which Anton had passed earlier and breathed a sigh of relief as he saw its arched windows, knowing his journey was soon coming to an end.

The oppressive migraine hit them both hard as Betty sat in a state of undress, watching a by-the-numbers procedural crime drama on their small cathode ray tube television. Fergus, also naked, was making a cup of tea in the kitchen. They both cried in agony and gripped their heads in anguish as the pain slammed into their minds. Unable to hold each other to find any comfort, they could only wallow in their own miserable agony. The rot had spread out from the street, and grew closer to their house as it infected their lawn, decorating the snow with its propagating death.

When it reached the walls of their house, Betty was the first to feel the heat from the inside of her stomach rise. The quickly advancing and searing pain in her head provided a deafening beat in her thoughts. As her guts started to boil in their own contained juices, she screamed as loud as she could for Fergus' help. Blood started to seep out of her groin and anus; First a drip or two, then more and more until it was akin to a tap being turned on. The warmth of her insides breaking out filled her with terror.

Fergus was in the same boat, gripping his stomach. He had fallen in the hallway as the headache first hit him, dropping the ornate china cup of boiling tea, spilling to the carpet beneath him. The rising pain then caused his legs to buckle as the scorching fiery agony took firmer hold.

With Betty still seated on their sofa, they were separated by a wall. Above the pain he felt, all Fergus could think of to do was get back to Betty, to make sure she was okay. His pain deafened him to her cries, so he had no idea she shared this same fate alongside him.

Crawling through the burning that coursed throughout his body, he tried to get back into the living room. To find his one love. Hoping whatever was happening would pass, and she could hold him in her arms

He would not be so lucky.

As he crawled at a slow, pained speed. He, like Betty, was now bleeding profusely from his nether regions, leaving a trail of blood, shit and bile behind him. Neither of them had even noticed the severity of what was happening due the searing torment their bodies now succumbed to.

As he got to the door way between the hallway and living room, he looked up. For one last time, he saw his Betty. The boiling inside her had reached fever pitch as she tried to scream once more, but her pulped and now liquefied insides erupted out of her mouth, eyes, nose and ears. A forceful torrent of blood, followed by a mashed-up matter from within her, spraying out all over the room. Jetting as if pressurised, it flooded out from her body. Together with this grotesque matter, followed the fragments of her bones that had collapsed within her. As she vomited up her entire insides, skeleton and all, her skin emptied as it vacated all its contents. Leaving the only shape of her in her legs, the rest of her body was now a mass of skin and expelled insides, slumped in a wet heap on the sofa.

In Fergus' eyes though, he saw it differently , He never saw the grotesquery of her demise. Instead, he saw simply her sitting in her chair, smiling seductively at him, naked as the day she was born. Beckoning him over as she parted her thighs.

A few moments later , not seeing the reality of his beloved's death and with a smile on his face from the delusions he witnessed, his insides followed the same path as hers. They spilled out from all orifices and billowed en masse out onto their carpet; mashed up bones and pulped muscles included.

House by house, this rot then visited. Throughout the whole of Folksville it went street by street, spreading its infection through the white snow to each building. Silently under the cover of the blizzard, it travelled without prejudice to any place the fallen white could host it and caused the same effect to any person its proximity chanced upon.

Men, women, dogs, babies, cat, gerbils, young, old, black, white, gay, straight, Christian, Atheist. Muslim. There was no preference or compassion within its effect. It was death, and it snaked through the town; a silent plague, indiscriminately snuffing out the life of everything it touched.

Within the space of an hour, the whole town had been covered by this presence. Where snow had dropped, the dark arms of this thing now reached. Where it had reached, it had infected everything.

With only the mountain left in its journey ahead, the rot was soon met by its foe; As the temperature dropped with each step of the progressing storm, its progression too had been slowed. This rot's increasing path now halted as the deeper, more brutal freeze began to set itself in. The crawling and spreading infection had been made to stop. Though not a cure that would kill this evil, the sub-zero temperature did not allow any more journey than the black mold had made already. As if it had permission to consume the town, but had not been allowed to consume the mountain , At least not at present.

It was the night before the burial of Henry Stacey and all through the town, not a creature was stirring, as they had all fallen down, dead. Liquefied from the inside. Not one thing was left living here. The lights may have still been on in the houses. The heating may have still warmed the rooms. The food may have still been on some plates. But the people and animals here all lay dead. Their bodies expelled of all their contents, spilled their mashed-up gore onto the floors around them. From this pulp, something grew; a mold, the same as the one enveloping the town. Growing from *within* their meat. Dark and grey, it spread through their blood and guts. Though the spreading rot outside had been halted by the freeze, inside , where it was warm , it now flourished. Covering each body with a thick dark fur. The air in the rooms, now rife with floating spores.

The only building in town untouched by this attack and the only building without people living in it, was the church of Jacob Stacey. When not in use, like tonight, it was a cold barren building. It had no heat when the services were not being held and even when they were, it was only heated by two old portable electric heaters which let out a weak warmth at the best of times. It had been the congregation's faith which provided their heat , That was what some of the townsfolk claimed anyway. Now it was the only building within the city limits that was not home to the rising disease, which had taken away the lives of the township.

On the streets themselves, underneath the thick snow which continued to beat down upon this recently deceased town, the rot

The Sacrifice of Anton Stacey

was now being hidden. As the volume of snowflakes covered the area thicker and thicker, the darkness of the halted killer was being disguised , until all that could be seen, when the light would return the next day, would be a beautiful image of a snow logged town. The underlying carpet of rot out of sight.

The following morning, unlike any other day after a huge snowfall, Jimmy Mons would not plow any of the snow from the streets. Normally he would have woken up at 3am, gotten in his snow plow, and driven around the town for hours and hours, clearing one section of the streets at a time. Over and over. Plowing the fallen debris as much as he could before sunrise. Even if the snow was still falling and recoating his recently cleared streets. He would continue to drive around until midday, waiting for people to flag him down, to pay him the 5 bucks he asked for to clear their driveways, or clear a certain path for them off the street. All of which he would happily oblige to do. On a bad day, he would earn a quick hundred bucks , but on his best day, nearly 500. Not bad for an ex-con without any education and only a knack with old machines to call a skill. He knew when he saw that plow in the junkyard that he could fix it up. and he was right. Best $50 ever spent. Without this, he had no idea where he would be. He *knew* the town hated him, and so they should. He hated himself in equal measure for what he had done. His pederast past had been atoned for in the eyes of the law, but not in the eyes of his neighbours, or more importantly to him, in the eyes of his God. So, he would spend each day just trying to earn a wage enough to live, to try to stay out of the hateful glare of the townsfolk as much as possible. He knew that those that flagged him down were either ignorant to his past, were kind enough to forgive, or just placed the state of their driveway above any morality they may pretend to cling to.

The only person in Jimmy Mon's life who showed him any degree of kindness, was the Pastor. The man who had loaned him the $50 that bought the plow. The man who gave him the tool set to fix it up. The man who, in return, only ever asked for the track between the cabin and the church be cleared if blocked. Of course, Jimmy would do this for him. Even after he paid back the money in full. He would do anything for this kind man. This man who did not even ask for him to attend the church, though he did anyway, with a smile. Even though he was not a Christian man and had to suffer the glare of the congregation, he went each Wednesday and Sunday. Sat at the back obediently. Then left before anyone else stood up , He owed the Pastor a *lot* for his kindness.

But this morning it would all change. The streets would stay snow-logged. The track to the church would not be made traversable by car. Jimmy's plow would remain under its protective sheet , and the town would not wake up again.

4

GOODBYE, APPALACHIA

Jacob had not slept through the majority of the night. With Anton finally being back in their shared childhood home, echoes of the past flooded his memory with a nostalgia and a want to relive the small glimpses of their shared past, which couldn't help but to make him smile; Like the time he and his brother played with some unwanted toys which were donated to the church, though the Pastor would not allow them to keep any, in order to keep them quiet, he would allow some toys to be taken home for the night. Only as long as there were no chores for them left to complete. Or like the one and only time which he saw his father look upon Anton with anything except disdain. These small glimpses of the past were enough to make him succumb to his insomnia for most of the night-time.

Though living in this cabin all of his life, it was his younger brother's proximity which gifted Jacob with long forgotten shadows of the past. Memories he had not thought of in decades.

After they had both polished off the entire bottle of cognac, they called it a night. Jacob was so happy to see his brother that his smile never left his face for the entire evening , No matter what the subject they covered was, and they talked solidly into the early hours. Even as he lay down unable to sleep, his face looked more content than it had done in years.

After the positive effects of the alcohol had crept away, it left Jacob with a dull ache in his head. The light from the ebbing fire still glowed throughout the room. Having willingly given up his own bed to his brother, he instead took the sofa. His mind too excited to sleep with recollections, despite the hangover now making its way into his body. There was too much in his thoughts to settle down. He hated to think that this evening was perfect and the best reunion he had hoped for, especially with their dead father being less than twenty feet away. But he had to admit the truth. *Lying to yourself is lying to the Lord*, as his sermons taught.

Outside, the wind continued to howl its banshee wail. The storm battered down onto the town, silencing the cries of the populous as they vomited up their entire lives. Hiding the rot which had crept, and now halted in its tracks halfway up the mountain to where he lay.

Making himself stand up, Jacob craved fresh air. Despite any weather conditions, he regularly stood on his porch in the depths of the night. Getting cold or wet never bothered him, he just enjoyed seeing the world when all others were asleep. He loved the feeling that he was the only one witnessing the miracle of Mother Nature.

Wrapping the bedsheet around his shoulder, he quietly walked to the front door and opened it, exited, then silently closed it behind him.

As he looked out from the porch, over the town, the snow was briefly letting up. Allowing Jacob to see the lights that remained on in the houses below. Strange at 4am, so many lights being on across the town, but nothing that caused him any concern. Maybe he had seen that before. He was too close to sleep to think much of it.

The only thing that was not normal here, was the lack of

Jimmy Mons and his plow working the streets. He would usually be out on a continual loop of the town, clearing the snow , Waiting for the people to wake up and get him to clear their drives. But again it was nothing he thought about too much.

His attention then turned to his own truck. The snow that had settled on it was thick and consuming. Hiding the windshield and all of its roof. Covering the coffin in the truck bed almost completely.

With his boots unlaced, having been thrown on his feet lazily, Jacob took a step out onto the track in front of the cabin. The snow reached up nearly 7 inches to his above his ankles.

Coming to a stop after a few paces, he looked upward, and closed his eyes, letting the pulsing blizzard cast its snowflakes upon his face. He had always called this moment his 'Angel Time'. A time of peace where it was just him and the silence of the world. Co-existing in a courtship of natural wonder.

Adjusting the bedsheet higher over his shoulders, he could feel the cold invading. Now standing at the edge of the track, looking over the sheer drop into the quarry before the town, he peered into the darkness below.

The rot that had eviscerated all life only a few hours before was in the throes of its freeze. The cold had halted its path, not far from where Jacob now stood. As the temperature dropped throughout the night, the sub-zero chill had stopped the rot's murderous molecules, one by one. Its crawl ebbing to a standstill within arm's reach of Jacob.

He squinted as the dull ache in his head became a bit sharper. Wincing at its progression, he turned to return inside. He had to try and get *some* sleep before tomorrow. Taking a coffin up to the mountain top was one thing, taking a coffin up to the mountain top in deep snow was another. Taking a coffin up to the mountain top in deep snow *with a hangover*. Well, they would see.

He was, though, happy that his father decided to release himself from this mortal coil during the winter of all seasons. Had it have been the summer, then all of this would have been and entirely different prospect. Especially as during the hotter days, the black bears would be out of their hibernation and would roam the forest looking for food. Though they did not pose the same danger that a Grizzly bear would, Black bears were still dangerous and could become quite problematic should you need to transport a dead body near to them. Other animals, despite the inclement weather, may make an appearance during any excursions, but they were of no bother. Deer, moose or skunk would run away at the first sign of an interloper. So, winter was preferable. Though, Jacob didn't envy the hard work of digging the grave in the icy dirt, but it *was* better than risking it in bear country.

Settling back on to this sofa, his head, still damp from the snowfall, rested on his pillow as he closed his eyes. The headache, though getting a bit worse was something he accepted. What did he expect after drinking half a bottle of cognac on an empty stomach, after all?

As the night took him for the last couple of hours of its life, Jacob slept a very deep and very happy sleep. He was so inescapably settled in his slumber, that he did not realise his nose trickled with blood, down his lip and onto the pillow, nor did he hear the strange scraping sounds coming from outside of the cabin. These are the sounds that woke Anton up in the bedroom for a brief moment.

Dozily lying in his brother's bed, he winced as his hangover bid him a sudden *hello* in its brazen fashion. The scraping sound from outside, now stopped, as his sleep snatched him away into unconsciousness again. In those fleeting moments when he was awake, he presumed the scraping sounds to be remnants from his last dream. But they were not.

The sunlight broke over the dead town of Folksville, as the darkness slithered away once more.

The houses below basked in the bright yet still freezing sunlight, as the blizzard left a trail of a light snow in its wake. Pausing before intending to return soon. The whole image was tranquil and beautiful. The lights from all of the houses remained switched on from the night before, and dulled in the light of the day. The streets were barren of any life that would normally be on them from the moment the night would leave.

Not today, though. Today the whole town was the graveyard; A graveyard covered in the frozen rot, hidden underneath the snow. The insides of each house, though, told a different tale. They were coated, floor to ceiling with the strange mold. Each heated room an incubator for this death.

The streets were now deep in a foot of snow and showed no immediate signs of melting. The freeze still clung to the streets like a new born to its mother. The temperature only looking to raise to -5 in a best-case scenario, and with no footfall to trample the snow, nor Jimmy Mons to plow. This town was now held within them moment of its own demise. Locked into that second. With its apocalypse now present, the town breathed no more. The only life for miles now rested in the Stacey cabin on the mountain side.

Within the house of Fergus and Betty, the rot had long since covered their now inside out remains, with a thick, black and furry substance. Today would have been these aging lovebird's anniversary. 5 years since they married. In the closet in the bedroom, hidden in one of his jacket pockets was a pair of air tickets to whisk the pair off to Maui in a couple of weeks' time; A place Betty always spoke of wishing to see before she died. Yet also a place which Fergus had no want to see within any part of his (now exposed) body. He hated the sun. Hated the beach. Hated tourist traps. Hated shorts. Hated it all. This was why they had never travelled to any tropical destinations together. But this trip was different. For his Betty, he would have sacrificed all of his wants for hers at any given opportunity, and had planned this trip for a couple of years. Waiting for the right time to show his declaration of love to her, which to him was the biggest thing he could offer her to symbolize his affection. However, he could rest easy knowing that they never had to go through with it , that their untimely deaths had halted him having to endure any kind of beach holiday. Betty, though, knew all about this surprise trip and deep within the pain of her grotesque demise, was happy enough even knowing that he would have done this for her. The trip being secondary to his declaration.

Like Fergus and Betty, the whole town was awash with unfulfilled dreams and dying regrets as the inhabitants lay in waste. The sun now dripped through the many window panes, through the glass not blocked out by the infecting rot which crawled upon them. This light shone in and rested upon the people's remains. All that was now left in these lives was silence. All their dreams and intents now forgotten in the mire of violence.

As the sun rose like a slumbering giant, not even birds could be heard to sing their songs on this particular winter's morning. The freeze encapsulated the town in its grip as the snow threatened to return from the clouds above. The next blizzard hid up there

The Sacrifice of Anton Stacey

somewhere, but did not yet show its face , for now it had left to grace somewhere else with its storm.

Up on the mountainside, a couple of hundred feet above the ground level, the old Stacey cabin sat nestled on the side of the dirt track, which ran from the base of the town, all the way up past the quarry. Eventually leading to the future area of Pastor Henrys interment.

Anton had woken up with a thump still present in his brain. The repetitive boom of his own heartbeat echoed sorely in his head. The alcohol had not been kind to him. He had never drunk cognac before, nor had he ever wished to drink it again, but the symbolism of last night's actions had been needed, thus the following hangover was an additional, yet acceptable, price to pay.

As he brushed his teeth, he looked at his reflection in the mirror. He was a child when he last stood here doing the very same thing. In this subdued lighting he had stared at himself twice a day throughout his childhood years, wondering what else there was for him. Wondering why his father hated him. Wondering who he really was under all of his masked anxiety. He would never had presumed the surreal path of fame, that fate would take him on. He now stood in the cabin where he grew up , Anton Stacey , Grammy award Winner. Oscar Winner. Winner of almost every other award for music out there. Back in the place that made him. Away from the burning glare of the spotlight. He smiled at the knowledge that he was a nothing here. He was anonymous , those who *did* know him, knew him as the Pastor's brother only.

Spitting out the remnants of the toothpaste into the sink, he ran the tap over his toothbrush, washing the minty foam away for the last time. He would never come back here. This was his final goodbye to the place. He would try to move his brother out to LA, but he would never travel back here to this town, no matter the reason. This town was the burial place of that version of Anton Stacey. A version long gone and gladly forgotten.

For one of the few times in his life, he started to sing one of his own songs as he got ready. The lyrics of which had been battering around his head, aching to escape since he got here, just as they did when he wrote them, on that bus ride away from here.

I leave the cold mountains, as they leave me
    A life I must escape with glee
    I love you, brother, but you must see
    Goodbye is what must be
    Our time has flown
    Goodbye Appalachia
    Farewell my friend
    Goodbye Appalachia
    Our time now the end
    Goodbye Appalachia
    I'll maybe come back again
    Goodbye Appalachia

He normally would never even think of his own songs in everyday life, but he had sung this particular refrain, like a mantra to himself, to help him get over the pain after running from his home. Now he sung it in apprehension of his second leaving. Hoping the lyrics would change to include his brother joining him.

Meanwhile on the sofa, Jacob had garnered an additional 78 minutes of sleep. Terrifying sleep filled to the mental brim with the vilest of nightmares. Sin after sin displayed in his dreamscape which had sent him waking up in a sweat covered panic. His headache ever present and ringing in his ears loudly. So loudly it

The Sacrifice of Anton Stacey

had affected his sight as he squinted to keep himself from vomiting or passing out.

As he stood from the damp bedsheets, his stomach knotted around itself and sent an increasing pulse of nausea throughout his body and into his throat. He thought to himself that this hangover was karmic payment for them insulting his father's ghost , by drinking what had been forbidden to drink. His thoughts then turned more panicked after he vomited with force into the toilet. Aside from the contents of his stomach being thrown out from within at incredible speed, so did blood. Blood that did not belong in his sick. About a cupful of congealed dark red mucus lay amongst the bile and stomach lining. The stench of the old cognac, half-digested food and coagulating blood hit his nose, sending him to vomit yet again. All until he was left retching nothing but air into the blood and vomit-soaked toilet bowl.

His back arched as his body tried to evacuate contents that had long been flushed away, till all that was left was a small trickle of blood dripping from the corner of his mouth. Sour copper was all he could taste. *Better than tasting vomit*, he thought to himself.

Washing his face in the sink, he looked at his reflection. *Cancer. It must be.* He thought to himself. *God dammit*. At a time like this, he considered blasphemy as acceptable. When not a party to Gods plan, the cruel aspects of life could seem evil and without purpose. So when stuck in the quagmire of doubt and fear, words were not a sin, but simply an exasperation of a purely human existence. Of course, this had happened many times before. Back twinge. *Cancer*. Sore eye. *Cancer*. Weird mark on his skin. *Cancer*. Hypochondria was a part of his molecular makeup. A fundamental part of him which he hid from everyone, everyone except his Marion. His confidante. His forbidden and presumably unrequited love. The one person he felt like a school child around , But he would not tell her about this. Normally it was the small things he spoke to her about. They both shared stories of their aging bodies getting stiffer and creakier, but he knew that vomiting blood was a tad more serious, and he didn't want her sympathy or sadness. His own worries aside, he and his brother had a busy day ahead of them. This worry could wait.

Outside the cabin, dressed in warm winter clothing, Jacob and Anton stood in the chilly white, both feeling quite ill. As his headache dimmed his energy, Jacob's chest felt the constant warm burning sensation within it , A signal of something being wrong. A signal he was choosing to ignore.

"This is a fucking dumb idea," Anton muttered.

"Can't say I disagree, little brother," Jacob smiled. "But, needs must as promises made."

Both of the brothers wore a mask of pretence towards each other, hiding their sickness as best as they could. Neither of them wanted to look weak or like their cognac escapade was a mistake. They were more or less strangers to each other, both not really knowing the heart of the other anymore , But only knowing the past and the letters they shared. Both not wanting to disappoint the other.

As they walked around the pick-up truck, the rear flatbed came into view.

"What in God's name?" was all Jacob could muster as they saw the rear door of the truck had been opened and the coffin dragged away. Off the metal shelf and onto the snowy track beneath it, it now lay on its side; the base of it facing the brothers.

As they approached this casket, the top of it revealed to have been ripped open. The coffin lid torn from its hinges, revealing the emptiness of its linen lined interior.

With no corpse of their father inhabiting it, the brothers looked speechless. Jacob had witnessed the lid of the coffin get screwed shut with long bolts. He saw the body of Pastor Henry

Stacey get sealed inside it. Now though, these screws had been ripped out from their resting places and the wood of the coffin lid lay splintered in two.

"You gotta be fucking kiddin' me," Anton's words barely as loud as his breath. He stared away from the coffin, tapped his brothers arm , requesting him to focus his attention in the same direction to which he now looked.

Turning to Anton, Jacob noticed the rising look of shock appearing on his brother's face, and turned to see what was filling him with so much horror.

They saw a mark in the snow leading away from the coffin, a mark of a body being dragged away. It had separated and flattened the settled snow which lay in its path, into the treeline a few meters away and toward the mountaintop. There were though, no other marks; No boot prints left from the villain who dragged the body away. Only the smeared mark left from the body itself.

"Tell me he didn't get up himself."

"I hope to Jesus Christ he didn't. This is," Jacob swallowed. "I don't know what this is."

"Bears?" Anton already knew the answer. The question came out of his mouth like a reflex.

"Hibernating," Jacob replied, confirming Anton's fears.

Glancing around, Jacob tried to look for any other clues on the ground. *Anything* to give them an idea of what happened.

Anton's attention turned briefly to the town below; The town which had no activity. No people milling around it. No cars driving down the streets.

The moment carried with it an eerie calm that both brothers could sense, yet chose to ignore.

"We better get the guns," Jacob said as he turned and walked back to the Cabin's open front door.

"Guns?" Anton asked surprised. "Really?"

Jacob heard this, then glanced back to his brother. "If somehow, you're right and it *is* a bear, he isn't gonna give up his dinner peacefully now, is he?"

As Jacob disappeared inside the cabin, Anton wondered why neither of them were panicking angrily, or screaming incoherently. Neither of them had the reactions he presumed they would have in this situation. He presumed that Jacob would have yelled, fallen to his feet praying for his God's guidance and intervention. Anton thought that normally, on any other day, he would have got into his car, screamed *fuck you* to Folksville and left this place in his dust. Yet here they both were, confused but calm. Some animal had probably ripped open their father's casket and dragged him away and the most he could muster was a bit of confusion and slight annoyance. That in itself should have been a warning sign.

Partially blaming his demeanour on his hangover, he looked again to the coffin; he could see no claw marks, no teeth marks, no tool marks. It looked as though the wood just splintered itself. Maybe it was his father back as a zombie to get revenge against them for drinking his cognac? He laughed silently at this thought , Picturing the man that he hated, now as one of the undead, stumbling through the mountain woodland moaning the word *conggggnnaaaaccc* instead of *brrraaaaiiiiinnnss*.

He realised his lack of emotion about this had a simple explanation; he simply didn't care at all for anything about that man. He was not here for someone who was only his father in a biological sense. He was here for the man who helped raise him. The man who taught him everything he knew. The man whom without, he had felt incomplete since leaving. He was here for Jacob. Here for his brother, to make amends for abandoning him many years ago. He couldn't give a witch's tit for what fate had befallen that awful man, Henry Stacey. Over the years since he escaped, his resentment and hurt had manifested itself into consummate hate. The memories of his past illuminated and framed his father's existence as an evil abusive man. A man whom fate had deemed so bad, it condemned him to a life of silent immobilised hell.

But though that explained his reaction, Anton wondered why Jacob of all people had been so matter of fact about it. He had taken care of that man for all of his adult life. Yet his reaction to his body going missing was to get guns?

Inside his home, as Jacob opened his gun cabinet, he thought about what had just happened and smirked to himself. Not out of humor, but from the ludicrousness of the situation itself. He had trouble focussing any hurt or worry at all; all of his concentration was focussed on masking the pain within his own body. He could still taste the blood in his throat, still feel the waves of nausea. It took everything to remain upright and not clutch his stomach in agony. He couldn't allow himself to be dragged into any emotional whirlwind about this. He had to stay focussed. Stay calm. Get through this. Find the body. Bury it. Allow his brother to leave. Then face whatever music was playing blaringly loud at him.

5

THE EYE'S DEATHLY LIGHTS

Anton and Jacob, having trekked up the snow-caked mountain track, now walked through the woodland gripping their rifles tightly. As they followed the trail of the dragged body, they both looked cautious and uncertain.

"Why the fuck are we even doing this?" Anton whispered.

With a look of distain, Jacob stopped for a moment and glanced sternly toward Anton. "You have to ask why we're tryin' to save our own father's body?"

"I'm not gonna die just to find it, we don't know what took it!" Anton protested.

"No one's asking you to die," Jacob said before continuing his slow hunt forward. "If there's trouble we won't hang around. I'm not selfish enough to give up, just cos he was an asshole."

Anton held his tongue. He didn't know if Jacob's words were aimed at him. Did his brother really think that he was selfish? Did he really think his leaving was his own fault? This all being too much, Anton quickly gave up his complaint and followed Jacob through the snow.

"Hold up," Jacob whispered as he raised his rifle at something laying ahead. Stopping in his tracks, Anton feebly lifted his rifle up mimicking his brother, but he had not held a weapon since he was last on this mountain, so had very little experience. Holding this gun made him feel no safer than not having one, as he didn't trust such an implement in his hands.

"What is it?" Anton asked quietly.

"Think it's a buck?" Jacob replied as he walked closer toward the dark lump on the ground ahead, that protruded from the deep snow at the base of an old tree. Anton followed a few steps behind and soon saw what his brother referred to. It *was* a deer. Though he could not see if it was a buck, he could see its burst eyeballs that dripped from its wide-open eyelids; these black holes stared out in horror, as its mouth lolled open. A dark deep stare Anton felt was accusatory. The longer he stared back into these pits, the more he started to feel a wave of unsteadiness , One that was amplified by his hangover. These vacant sockets shot daggers toward him, as they blinded his other senses with their emptiness; consuming him. It was the strangest nausea he had ever felt. Caused by a darkness that made it difficult to focus on any other of his other senses.

"Anton?" Jacob shouted aloud for the second time. "Hey, brother!" he called out yet again , This time catching Anton's attention away from the eyeless stare.

"Huh?" he said wearily as he looked at Jacob.

"You okay?" Jacob asked. "You don't look too good."

Shrugging off the dread feeling now coursing through his body, he smiled as he walked round the deer to his brother's side. "I'm okay, must have been the cognac, I guess."

"Tell me about it. I got rattlesnakes in my belly," Jacob smiled as he nodded to where they were going. "Tracks seem to end up there." He nodded, noticing that the drag marks they were on the trail of, stopped short of a large old tree which rested on a ridge leading further into the mountain woodland. "Let's take a look."

"And then what?" Anton enquired.

"Guess we go back to the police and get *them* to search."

"Okay," Anton replied as they then walked cautiously to the tracks end. He just wanted to run away. Everything in his entire being was screaming at him that something was wrong and things would not end well in this place. They never had and they never would.

"God's mercy," Jacob whispered as he spotted the corpse of another deer. Lying on the other side of the tree, in the same state as the larger one they just happened upon; Devoid of life, without any eyes and carrying with it, an entrancing dead stare.

"I know I asked this before, but, a bear?" Anton asked. His brothers attention was now away from this deer and looked to the other side of the treeline on the ridge. He motioned with the barrel of his rifle to the fallen doe. "You hang back for one second, okay?" he said as he walked towards the ridge.

"What?" Anton weakly protested "I'm not staying here on my own."

Glancing back, Jacob reiterated sternly "Just one second."

As he approached the second deer, Anton couldn't help but down at its corpse. This situation disturbing him more with each moment. But before he could complain more to his brother, to try and speaks some sense into him, that they should leave, Jacob was gone , Already having walked over the ridge.

As Anton stood alone at this trail's end, the silence started to build. He avoided the dead eyed gaze of the deer at his feet, and instead glanced upward, through the trees to the gray skies above. The skies which threatened to release more snowflakes. Lying in wait until it could send more dancing white downward, to join their icy kind on the woodland ground.

On the other side of the ridge, Jacob looked in shock at what he witnessed. Around this wide clearing, dozens of dead animals littered the ground as far as he could see. All had their eyeballs burst wide open, with the jelly from within now scattered across

The Sacrifice of Anton Stacey

the pure snow in front of them. Foxes, deer, scores of birds and even a brown bear , All had fallen at the same time. All faced the same direction, as if they had been running away, or had been chased by something.

Taking a few tentative footsteps deeper into the clearing, he pulled his rifle in closer to his shoulder. He steadied his grip as best he could, despite his headache violently banging and his chest burning painfully. He focused with as much determination as he could muster. Despite the pain getting worse, he had to carry on.

Taking a few more paces, he quickly sensed a presence standing behind him. Spinning around he aimed his gun directly , at nothing. There was nothing behind him except the many dead animals. He scanned the area behind him to make sure. Tracking from left to right along the rifle barrel.

Turning back, he carried on his scouting of the area. As he walked past the large dead bear, he noticed, that lodged in its claws were sizable clumps of flesh. As he wondered how anything woke a hibernating bear, something out of the corner of his eye drew his attention. About twenty feet away, he noticed a mass. His attention now focused. Filling with dread he tried to force himself to keep his eyes open, and not turn away. *He knew what was there.* Underneath a blossoming evergreen, a black suited figure slumped in a seated position on the ground. The snow, covering it like a blanket, did nothing to hide what it was. Jacob's heartbeat quickened. The spit in his mouth, dried up. Trying to swallow, the lump in this throat would not leave. His stomach turned as he saw the figure's suit was split open down its back , as only a body dressed for a coffin would wear.

Though Jacob could only see from the rear, he already knew it was the remains of his father. He could see the blue socks sticking out of the patent leather shoes on the legs that spread out from the figure. *It must be him*, he thought, *besides, in this town, how many bodies in a funeral cut suit and blue socks were missing on this damn mountain?*

Though the clearing was silent and calm, he kept in the forefront of his mind that what did this could still be around , laying in wait for its next victim. With this in mind, he walked cautiously up to the front of the seated corpse with his rifle held up defensively.

As he glanced down at the body, he quickly closed his eyes in repulsion. Its face had been chewed clean off. The skull had been caved in from huge gouging teeth marks. The chest shredded with large claw marks around it. Looking back to the dead brown bear nearby, he grimaced.

That had to be the culprit.

His brother was right.

That was what took his father.

"Hope you choked on it, you bastard," he uttered quietly at the dead animal.

Anton, far on the other side of the ridge, swallowed his fear as best he could. He had been fighting the urge to vomit, but lost the battle on the other side of the tree. Noticing some blood in his bile, he fell into a deep well of anguish. His nausea and headache were worsening, and being out here didn't help. He would be going home today. No matter *how* bad he felt, he *had* to get out of Folksville and back to the City that championed him.

"Anton!" echoed Jacob's voice from over the ridge. Loud and commanding. "Quickly, get over here!" he continued.

Why the fuck was he shouting? Anton thought to himself, bringing him out of his maudlin sickly state.

Walking past the second dead deer, he walked up and over to the ridge. Ahead of him lay a second ridge, which he walked up to and looked over. In the clearing beneath him, he saw Jacob. His gun now resting by his side. His expression forlorn.

"Everything okay?" he called out.

To which Jacob's wide-eyed gaze shot toward Anton. "Shhhhhh!" hissed his reply.

Confused, Anton walked over the second ridge and down to his brother. "What d'ya mean shhhh? You called me!" he said quieter.

"Call you? I didn't call you," Jacob stared at him confused. "I told you to stay there!"

"You *just* called me," Anton repeated, ignoring his brother's denial.

"You should go back. You don't wanna see the Pastor like this," Jacob said, his eyes wet from a build-up of emotion.

"See him? Where?" Anton asked as he looked around at the barren clearing. It now only being populated by trees, snow and their footprints.

Jacob's eyes widened as looked around and now saw as his brother did. Nothing was here anymore. No bear. No father. No other animals. "He *was* here," he said weakly as his voice wavered. "He was right here."

A sharp and insurmountable pain then shot through Jacobs torso, as the rising burning feeling now surged with fury. Gritting his teeth and screaming the best he could, he collapsed to his knees, onto the snowy ground.

"Jacob!" Anton exclaimed in a panic and he grabbed his brother's shoulders, trying and failing to catch him as he fell. Jacob's eyes were closed tightly from the pain.

"What's the matter?" Anton worriedly shouted over his brother's screams.

Jacob's whole body tensed as he tried to push the pain down. Tried to supress its control of him. With teeth still gritted he looked to his brother through the welling tears. "Get. Help. Please."

"I can't leave you," Anton fearfully pleaded to his brother. "I'll carry you down, okay?

Moving to pick his brother up, Anton lifted one of his Jacob's arms over his shoulder. As he did, the pain in Jacob's chest returned with more force, as its heat cut though his lungs, causing him to scream even louder. Blood dripping from his mouth.

Knowing he had no other choice than to leave to get help, Anton stopped his attempts to move his brother. "Okay, I'll be *right* back! Okay?"

Jacob's body hunched over in agony. Through the spittle and blood that dripped down from his mouth and despite the battering his body was experiencing, he the glanced to his brother, terrified, and managed to say "Hurry, please, hurry." The pain then overtook him, as he hunched onto the ground into a foetal position and gripped his chest.

Sprinting over the ridge, Anton had not noticed that the two dead deer they had seen before were also missing. As if never being there in the first place.

After a minute or two passed, the pain which shot through Jacob's body was slowly loosening its grip. His breathing was returning to normal as his heartbeat started to slow down to its regular rate. The pain for some reason retreated and his body was left feeling the cold of not only the snow that he lay on, but also from inside his body as well. The searing heat that was there, now freezing.

Wiping his eyes with the back of his hand, he looked forward and saw that, once again, death had returned to the scene. His father's decimated body sat slumped, faceless. The dead bear and other animals were also where they lay before.

Staggering to his feet, he tried to concentrate more on getting out of this place, to catch up to his brother. He blocked out the thoughts his mind threw at him, of the reappearance of these

The Sacrifice of Anton Stacey

animals and his father. The insanity that filled this place pushed to the background, along with the pain he felt was about to kill him.

He could only think of Anton. He tried to scream his name, but little sound came out. He did not have the strength or the breath to say much of anything, let alone scream to a man running away a minute in front of him.

He staggered to his feet, clutching his chest and turned to follow Anton's path back.

As quickly as he had stood, he fell to his knees again, as his eyes were filled with the sight of something now standing only a few feet away, directly in front him.

The figure stood over nine feet tall and stared down at him in utter silence. Jacob's eyes strained to see it more clearly, but it wasn't his eyes that were the issue; the figure was a living blur. It was also naked, from what he could tell. From its back, a pair of large red wings protruded, open as wide as this form was tall. Liquid resembling blood dripped from these wings from a blurred state and into the snow below.

Jacob knelt wide-eyed and in awe of what he was witnessing.

The pain he had felt was now only a distant numbness within him.

"Save the souls, disciple," came a booming voice from this being. It then looked upward to the sky, stretched out its arms and continued. "The world in blood demands its balance, and I give your body peace."

A smile of awe and wonder slowly crept over Jacob's weathered face. His eyes welled with tears, as he noticed the pain throughout his body was now a distant memory. Gone from agony to numbness to now nothing.

"I, I am your humble servant," he said quietly through his adulation, knowing this was heaven sent.

The red glow from this figure started to brighten as it its gaze met Jacobs. "Follow the signs. Exorcize the demons at the feet of the Lord on high." It said.

The words seeped into Jacob's brain, as he basked in the blood tinged illuminations of what he believed to be an angel.

As this being towered over him, he felt a warm comfort , like what he presumed was akin being held in a lover's embrace, not that he ever had experienced that. The pure feeling of love washed over him. Tears escaped down his cheeks en-masse as he felt his God's presence.

The being's blood wings rose higher, before it repeated it's imperative; "Follow the signs."

Anton ran through the fallen snow and undergrowth of the mountain woodland , About half the distance from between Jacob and the cabin. He had about another mile to go. Then it would be another half mile down a snow-logged track, if he was to go to the now dead town of Folksville to try and find the police, or an ambulance, or whatever he could.

Losing his breath, he slowed for a moment. Coming to a stop in order to regain the energy that had escaped him on his journey down so far. Despite having a personal trainer back in LA, despite exercising daily, he had no stamina. He had only ever done the bare minimum. Enough to make sure he didn't have a heart attack, but not enough to build up any muscle or burn fat. Today, he wished he had listened to his trainer. Done the exercising asked.

His legs burned with pain from the over exertion from the descent on uneven terrain. His lungs felt like he had smoked a hundred cigarettes the night before. His breath was loud as he tried his best to reject the agony he felt. To break through this exhaustion and get his brother help.

Moving again, with his breath barely caught, he staggered on. His footsteps heavy, and slower from when he started.

His head pounded from the blood coursing through his veins, trying to deliver oxygen to his body , Trying to do all it could to obey his brain's command to run as fast as possible. His booming heartbeat echoed in his head and eclipsed any other sounds of the wild , Not that there were any other noises. Had he been of a mind to consider the noises that were there, he would have seen that there was no noise apart from the wind. No critters making their squeaks. No birds making their songs. Nothing. No cars sounded from the town. No noise at all, anywhere.

The pain he felt earlier was still present, but now joined with the chorus of pain that the running had caused him. It was now one indiscernible mass of torture.

"Anton!" came a long echoing call from far behind him. Not hearing it at first, it wasn't until Jacob's third call of his brother's name, that Anton slowed down. "Anton!" his name echoed down the mountainside again. Turning around he could only feel relief. His brother had enough strength to call loudly? He must be okay. Whatever happened must have gone, at least for now.

"I'm down here!" Anton shouted back as best he could, but it was weak. What he intended as a shout came out as an exhausted wheeze.

"I'm coming to you," came Jacob's reply as he sounded clear and healthy. He couldn't be that far away, Anton thought to himself as he smiled. His hands fell onto his thighs as he bent down in order to catch his breath.

After a few moments, something grabbed his attention. Standing up again, with his breath slowly returning to normal, his eyes focussed beyond the snowfall ahead of him. He looked toward a part of the woodland just off the track from where he stood; to where three old fallen trees lay across a gorge in the ground. Something he had not noticed on their journey upward. Something he should have remembered was here. *The treehouse*, he thought with a smile.

Walking toward it he could see, despite the thick layer of snow which covered it, the door to their hideaway. A door which they had gotten from Ross Perkins, the local carpenter. Hearing they were building a treehouse, he had offered them offcuts in exchange for some chores that he had been avoiding, painting the store, making deliveries, as well as anything else he deemed to be assistants work. So, over the course of one summer, they did just as he asked. Delivering wood on a trolley to various customers across town. Stained fence panels. Badly gave his shop a second lick of paint. They had spent the best part of three months helping Mr Perkins in any way they could, all whilst avoiding the radar of the Pastor. He would be furious if he had known they were working for a man who was not part of his congregation. Nevertheless, the Stacey Brothers spent all their spare time earning enough to get the door and wall panels they needed to build their treehouse, all made to the dimensions that Jacob had measured under the fallen trees.

As Anton walked nearer, he could see that the wood panels still stood strong, still looked in good condition.

The window to the door was aged and blackened from neglect and the passage of time, but could still be glanced through to the inside. Peering in, Anton could see the small wooden seats they got from the trash cans at the gas station, the shelving unit they found in the junk yard, even the oversized mirror they put against the far wall still stood there. Though aged and dirty, it still displayed his reflection clearly. The lacquer on all the walls had protected them from the elements. The trees which lay above them, though fallen, still provided them with a solid and protective roof. The undergrowth though did not keep away. Over the decades, it had worked its way into that sanctuary they had built and filled its insides with thick branches and foliage. The far side window to the treehouse had been smashed from a branch breaking through it and now doubled as an entrance for any small animals in the forest to walk through. Anton liked the idea that they may use their hideaway to mate, hibernate and build a den in. *At least someone made it a home!* he mused.

"Brother," Anton heard from behind him. Turning he was met with the smiling almost rejuvenated face of his older sibling. "I see you found the fortress." His voice almost creepy in how well it sounded.

Anton walked up to him and looked intently into his eyes. "You ok? What happened?"

"Everything happened, my brother. Everything I could dream," came his vague reply.

"What was it? How are you feeling?" Anton asked rapidly as a mild panic crept in. His brother had been debilitated and somehow was now walking and smiling less than twenty minutes later. "You need to sit down?" he asked as Jacob just smiled back to him.

"Cease any worry, God is here for us," Jacob's smile opened up to show his white teeth as a big welcoming grin spread over his face.

"God is what?" Anton replied in confusion. "Look, you need to see someone. A doctor or someone."

"God was everywhere, you know," Jacob said smiling. "In the clouds, in the air, in the depths of the earth. But now," his smile slightly dropped as he continued. "Now, He's right here to give us His word. I saw His angel, Anton. I saw His message."

Worry filled Anton as he heard those words about God, but it was not just what was said that worried him, but also how his brother now looked; Despite being the larger of the two, Jacob had also been the more sickly child. Growing up through harsh winters did nothing to strengthen any immunities like it did Anton, who even as a small child was rarely tired, let alone sick. When he arrived from LA the day before, he had noticed that Jacob was the same as he was decades before; pale, gaunt and frail. Yet now, standing on this mountain, Anton regarded his brother , Who now looked strong and healthy, with a warm color flushing his cheeks , as if this experience had given him strength that his life had denied him until now.

Grinning, Jacob stood with this renewed vigor, talking about angels. Anton had no other option than to be concerned for him; Having just seen him in so much pain , he had to get him to a doctor, whether he was looking as healthy as ever or not. *Something* was wrong.

Of course, he knew his brother believed in God. He was a Pastor after all, but there was a difference between preaching the good word, and explicitly saying you *just* saw an angel , Especially only moments after he was clutching his chest and screaming in agony for help.

"Just do me this one favor," Anton asked as he put one hand on his brother's shoulder, "angel or not, come with me to the doctors. Just to check you out. What happened up there was just not a little thing, okay? You saw things up there. The Pastor. Now an angel? I.. I'm not doubting you. I just wanna make sure."

"That was all just a test, my dearest brother. The rest is nothing. I'm fine. I feel strong and well," Jacob's words fell over his lips as he blinked for a few moments, taking in the moment.

A smattering of snowflakes re-emerged from the clouds and started to fall upon them. A flurry of flakes dancing around them in this peaceful clearing. "Besides," Jacob said, "You heard my voice calling you, when I said nothing. So why aren't you hurrying to get looked at?"

The Sacrifice of Anton Stacey

"I will. Please, let's just go check."

"First, let's get back to the cabin before we catch a death, okay?" Jacob said, as he put one arm around his brother's shoulders.

"Please Jacob, just see a doctor?"

He knew that his little brother would not let this go. "Fine, we can go to town. But only on one condition. We leave what happened up here, up here. As far as they should be aware, we buried our father."

"You don't want them to know about it?"

"Despite your doubt, I *did* feel the purity of His word. This was all in the plan. Everything I saw , All part of it. So, I ain't gonna doubt it."

"The dead animals? The hallucinations. I think we're both sick," Anton said as he tried to talk logic. "Connect the dots. This isn't God, this is something else. A pathogen? A chemical attack? I don't know. But something is wrong."

Jacob stopped for a moment, looking disturbed at Anton's disbelief. "I understand your worried brother, but don't disparage my faith with that talk. A Pathogen? Where's that even coming from? My belief is based on thousands of years of theological understanding. Your whole opinion is based on paranoia and fear. Without any faith, you're empty of the capacity to see this beautiful truth."

"I, I'm not. I'm just saying all those things have to be linked. They're signs we can't ignore."

Pausing for a moment, Jacob looked at his brother and closed his eyes briefly. With a sense of calm, he said, "Signs. You're right, they *are* signs, and I *will* understand them," he turned to walk back down the mountain track, with his arm still around his brother.

"You'll see the doctor, right?" Anton asked again sheepishly.

"Let's go to town," Jacob replied looking ahead "But don't expect me to kowtow to any blasphemy, okay?"

. . .

As they walked down the mountain at a slow pace, there was no more conversation between them. Jacob happily hummed a hymn to himself as he looked out over the beautiful vista of the township below. He relived the meeting of divinity which he was positive had happened. He still heard those angelic words. He was determined he would see signs that were demanded. He would send any demons straight back to hell. At this moment, he felt something he had not felt in a long time; righteousness and a holy cause. He would do everything in his power to follow the divine commands given.

As he walked slowly beside his humming brother, Anton could only feel the pangs of anxiety eating away at his core. Something *had* affected them both. His headache was still present, as was the nausea sloshing within his stomach. With the morning leaving and the daytime approaching its infancy, he could sense that this wasn't alcohol induced any more. He had drunk enough alcohol and experienced enough hangovers to realise that it was not what he felt. He *did* hallucinate hearing his brother's call as well as felt a chronic sickness and vomited some blood , So, if they *were* exposed to something, Jacob had been exposed much more than he had been.

It *had* to be something on the mountain.

It had to be.

His mind kept going back to his brother's belief in seeing an angel. His brother was not an evangelical man. He had faith and taught the scriptures, but claiming to see visions had never been a part of his repertoire. Not the boy he grew up with, not the man in the letters. In the back of his thoughts, he hoped his brother *was* sick, as if he indeed was the kind of person to believe this, then he was not the man he thought he was.

Everything from this morning had filled him with an extreme sense of dread. A dread which manifested itself incrementally since the moment that he stared into the black light of the deer's dead eyes.

6

THESE ROTTEN STREETS

As the sun began to set early, the snow fell harder upon the deathly silence in Folksville. As the moon became visible, the bitter cold began to set in once more.

Taking the pick-up truck down the mountain track would be nigh on impossible considering the amount of snow that had fallen over the past few hours. Without Jimmy Mons' plow, there was no other option for the brothers, but to walk down to the streets on foot.

The half-mile downward seemed twice as long as it was, as Jacob and Anton traversed the icy patches and walked through the deep untouched snowfall. Not knowing of the frozen rot beneath their feet.

Jacob walked and never took his eyes off of the town that lay at the bottom of their journey. The silence that echoed from below was, to him anyway, a sign that he must follow. *Follow the signs*. And that was exactly what he was doing.

He knew how it all sounded. He wasn't dumb. He knew that seeing an angel in the flesh was not something people would believe, should he choose to tell them, nor should they. He fully expected the scorn that came from his brother. The one who, on many occasions, wrote about his lack of faith within the pages of their correspondence. Though always apologetic about offending his brother with his opinions, Anton never realised that Jacob was not like his Father in that respect, as he did not care if others chose not to believe or believed something else. He was a Pastor to preach to the converted and accept anyone who *wished* to listen. That was all. He knew God was forgiving, and would accept any good person who may come into His grace. It did not matter if they believed in Him or not.

The unspoken tension between Anton and Jacob hung heavily. This oppressive quiet only occasionally broken by Anton's inquiry into Jacobs health; *Are you ok? How's your chest feeling? Is your arm numb? Can you smell burnt toast?* With these seemingly random questions, he was convinced that there was not any heart attack or stroke in the offing. Though not a doctor, he believed his Google-fed knowledge afforded him some intellect, though he had no idea of the exact reason behind those questions, he just knew to ask them. But when there were no words spoken, the air between them was uncomfortable, as if a fight was about to break out. Though there was not.

In the rest of the silence Anton considered other causes to their conditions and situation; Poisoning? The nearby lake had seemingly dried up without any of the townsfolk noticing, there were dead animals, hallucinations, searing pain, delusions, nausea. There was too much here to not be linked to a singular cause. Coincidences of events *this* close together, were improbable, though not impossible.

The brothers now stood on the main drag into town. The approaching night-time was only a mask for how early in the day it was. 4pm looked like 9pm in this deep winter landscape.

The street which in places had been caked in nearly 2 feet of snow. Snow that was undisturbed since it started to fall late last night.

They stood looking into this ghost town as the deathly silence seemed to stare back at them.

As well as not seeing the rot that lay frozen beneath their feet. The rot which destroyed all the town's life. Neither did they see the rot which now blossomed within the still-warm houses, nesting and covering the interior walls and floors of each of the rooms , flowering with its dark brown thorny buds over the bodies of those it had decimated. Anton was too busy looking for help for him and his brother, and was not concerned with looking into people's windows. Of course he was curious to where everyone was, but carried on down the street to where the main throng of stores were.

"Town usually like this?" Anton asked.

"No," Jacob looked around with a semblance of worry. "It sure isn't usual."

Anton moved over to the clear sidewalk, which had been protected from the snowfall by a large glass awning, which ran overhead down the full length of the storefronts on this street.

"Hey," Anton called back to his brother. "Doc's still down this way?"

"Nothing's changed that much," Jacob nodded as he trod carefully through the deep snow, over to his brother on the virtually snow-free sidewalk.

Looking into the stores as they walked past, Anton noticed that nothing was open as should have been. With no one alive to open up their doors or to turn the lights on, each of these storefronts were left dark, cold and foreboding. He started to wonder about the gravity of the situation they were in. If there was a correlation between the lack of people and their predicament. If he *had* looked into their windows as he walked by their houses, he would have been one step closer to the answer. Because of this he paused

The Sacrifice of Anton Stacey

as he looked around, realising that the doctors may not be the most advisable first port of call.

"Actually, hold on the doctor. Sheriff station should be open though, right? They never close up?" Anton asked trying to mask the worry in his voice.

Instead of nodding and confirming that the sheriff's station was indeed open 24/7, Jacob was frozen to the spot a few feet behind and could only stare at a new visitor standing nearby.

He saw that beside Anton, no more than a couple of feet away, was a dark pulsing shadow. A moving shadow. A living shadow. Undulating every second of its existence. This shape had crawled across the sidewalk on all fours, until it stopped in its tracks beside Anton. Deep within its shadow lay two glowing blue eyes which stared intently directly at Jacob.

"What the matter?" Anton asked, as he looked behind himself to where his brother stared, now slack jawed with fear , but he saw nothing.

Jacob heard a familiar voice from behind him, "You have nothing to fear, disciple."

Turning, he saw the red angel stood at the far end of the street, where the dirt track up the mountain began. Though more than a football field away, Jacob heard its words as though they were whispered directly into his ear.

"You are protected against this darkness," it continued.

"Jacob? What's wrong?" Anton enquired again, as he now stood beside his brother, grabbing him by the arm.

Jacob turned from the direction of the angel to glance at his brother, who stood waiting for his answer. Ignoring it, he just turned back.

Now standing in his way, having moved silently out of view, the shadow demon stood between him and the divine apparition.

The dark presence lifted a thin and gnarled looking arm and

motioned to the street beside him. A small giggle emanated from its maw as Jacob's eyes widened.

The veil had been lifted some more, as he noticed that littering the area, presumably materialized by this force, the snowy ground was now strewn with corpses of what appeared to be the townsfolk. Hundreds and hundreds of them. Each of these dead bodies carried with them a wide-eyed expression of screaming fear. Each of their mouths were distended as wide as possible , Not one of them expressed an expected peaceful look of someone who experienced a painless death. Each and every one of these scores of corpses, all faced in Jacob's direction. The dark presence now glided over the bodies in its path, as it slowly walked closer to them, all the while it still emitted its lascivious giggle.

"*Jacob!*" Anton screamed, trying to get his brothers attention as he shook him by his shoulders.

Jacob snapped back to reality, and to his brother with a look of fear. "You. You can't see them, can you?" Jacob asked, still in shock.

"Who?" Anton looked around, only to see an empty town. "Let's get help, okay?" He turned to walk towards the sheriff's station.

"No," Jacob said with fear, as he heard words from the angel.

"What do you mean, No?" Anton asked as he looked back, then realizing that his brother was speaking to someone else, not him.

"I can't. Please, don't ask that of me," Jacob pleaded with little volume.

Anton looked concerned, then glanced up and down the street looking for the Sheriff's station. He knew it was here somewhere, but his memory was not what it once was. The town here all seemed familiar, but it was more like a dream, than a distant reality.

"There!" he said relieved as he noticed the Sheriff's station sign just up ahead of them. "Stay here, okay? I'm goin to get help," he asked of Jacob as he turned and ran towards the answers that he wished to find.

"He's a good man. Anton is a *good* man. I swear it," Jacob gently sobbed.

Inside the Sheriff's station, nothing stirred. The doors were open, but no life could be seen. No lights were on. No heating.

"Hello?" Anton called out. "Anyone here?"

There came no reply.

There *were* two people here when the rot hit. The deputy sheriff and the receptionist. A couple who had been, when the rot struck through them, in one of the empty cells within the basement, deep in the haze of copulation. The deputy's insides burst out of him, forcing themselves into her body as he climaxed at his moment of internal liquidation. In turn, with her climaxing at the same second, her bones, flesh and sinew exploded from out of her mouth. Leaving them in a conjoined mass of skin and gore, connected together. Forever.

Without even considering to look downstairs within the cells, Anton turned back around and out onto the sidewalk. His brother now walked across the middle of the street looking around at the dead bodies only he could see. In his mind he saw them all staring back at him. Their bodies still, yet their eyes seemed to move in whatever direction he chose to walked in.

"Hey!" Anton called out, not yet feeling the agony that was about to grip him. Like his brother had experienced on the mountain, a searing pain soon shot through him in a heartbeat and forced him to his knees, overcoming him as he hit the icy asphalt.

As he began to cry, the tears felt thicker and warmer than normal. He touched his face with a shaking hand, and saw that his finger came away streaked in red. He was crying blood.

"*Jacob!*" He screamed in a tormented panic, calling for his brother. Forgetting the insanity of the day, all he could think of was needing his older sibling. Needing some, any help.

As he fell into unconsciousness, Anton saw, through the blood pooling in his eyes, Jacob rushing over shouting, "*Fight it! The angel HAS to be wrong. I know you can beat this evil, I don't want this test!*"

If Anton had been awake for a few moments longer, he would have heard something which would have chilled him worse than the coldest of temperatures could.

"*NO! I can't! You can't make me!*" Jacob pleaded to the invisible angel. "*You can't make me hurt him. Please NO!!! Ask him, please! Give me any other test of my devotion!*"

7

THE ASCENSION OF ANTON STACEY

In the darkness of Anton's mind, various muffled sounds started to become clearer in definition; The echoed footsteps which at first were vague thuds now sharpened as they approached him. Slowly, other surrounding noises started to form into more familiar and distinguishable events. The unconsciousness he had fallen into had been so deep and seemingly inescapable, that climbing his way out from it had been no easy, nor quick task.

Within the blackness which stole him away, he had dreamt of his father; Pastor Henry Stacey. The man who was a regular character within his dreamscapes. Usually presenting himself as a monster that chased him, the Pastor was never a kind figure but only a caricature of Anton's fear. This dream though, was different. The dream he had now, was one of simple recollection. With no exaggerated aspects within, it was a basic retelling of a past event. The event where Henry Stacey drove both of his sons many miles to the next town, so they may all go to the cinema as a family. That was the only time he would take them there, or anywhere else for that matter, as the rest of their childhood was squarely based in the limits of their provincial mountain town. This trip was the singular most happy memory Anton had of his father; Watching that cartoon bear singing about eating ants, became a defining moment in the young Anton's life, a moment which he hated to remember. A memory of his father being anything but a monster humanized him too much. It was easier him being remembered as 100% evil. Not 1% good. But in *that* cinema, he looked up as he laughed and saw his father laughing too. When his father then caught his eye, he leaned in and said "I'm sorry I'm not the best father. I'm going to change." This confession was retracted and short lived the next time he deemed them to be ungodly or believe their behaviour deserved his belt. His harsh demeanor, which had been imposed on them on a daily basis was within this dark cinema in respite, but such a lull would never be repeated or even discussed again.

As the cold crept through the warmth of his coat. Anton could feel that he was laying on a hard, stone surface. He could only presume he was still on the sidewalk. He heard his brothers voice from above him, muttering words in a foreign language and in monotonous tone, "*Too salvum me fac, et virtúte tua age causam meam. Deus, audi oratiónem meam; áuribus pércipe verba oris mei. Nam supérbi insurréxunt contra me.*"

As Anton grappled to escape his unconsciousness, he felt a stirring from within him; a gnawing unease about his situation. This, coupled with the pain which still dwelled in his head and stomach made for an unbearable cocktail, which all now came into a sharp focus, as the moonlight crawled over the stone surface, hitting his eyelids and dragging him into the waking world.

As he forced his eyes to focus, the blood red tears still coloured his view. He could see that he was no longer on the street, but in the place he never wanted to return to; his father's church. Candles lined the altar, upon which he found himself bound with thick twine. . The surrounding walls carried with them a slight

The Sacrifice of Anton Stacey

blackening. The rot which had crawled throughout the town less than 24 hours earlier, now crept slowly and silently towards where they were. When Jacob had walked in an hour before and switched on the oil heaters, the temperature started to rise just enough to allow the frozen killer which lay in wait outside, to being its thaw and follow its way on the hunt for more victims.

Anton lay on the altar in confusion as he tried his best to wriggle free of his bindings , In his weakened state it was futile.

He was secured tightly and inescapably.

"Shhhh, sweet brother," Jacob said kindly as he looked down at Anton. Now dressed within his Pastor's robes, his face looked gaunter than it had before. His pallor was now ashen and his lips, yellow. Though not in pain, standing and talking, Jacob did not look well. Gone was the healthy look he seemed to magically gain on the mountain. Now was a complexion of a very ill man. In his hand, he weakly held an old book, which was open to the page where he continued to read from in a mumble, "*et violénti quasi-érunt vitam meam.*"

"I need a doctor," Anton pleaded. His words cut through his dry throat, with pain. Each word said felt like a dagger cutting into him. "You need one too. Please. You don't look well."

Having paused reading, Jacob glanced down to Anton with a kindly smile, "You only need God's help. You will see, I have come to accept everything for what it is." came his reply.

"What? Please, let me go."

Looking back down to his book, Jacob's smile dropped. "I *had* to bind you," he said with a waver in his voice. "You've been taken by the dark one. It's a test you see? So I may prove my worth and save this world. You *will* be saved, so will *everyone*. You will see. Que Será Será little brother."

Anton, meanwhile, was at a loss for words, as he stared at his sibling.

"It is why you couldn't see His grace. You were chosen to be the vessel for the darkness instead. So it may be laid to rest," Jacob continued. "You started to see God on the mountain, but then, you were deemed chosen for this greater honor. So, it took you," he then started to mumble, reading from his book again, "*Non proposuérunt-*"

"*Let me fucking go!*" Anton screamed, cutting off his brother's words, with a sudden burst of energy.

After closing his eyes for a brief second, Jacob looked back at his brother. "The demon inside you talks solely with fear and anger. You need no more proof than that of its presence. God's test is about love and acceptance. If I succeed, *if* I do this, *everything* will be saved. You must realize that *I have no choice.*"

"You gotta see this isn't right," Anton pleaded. "Jacob?"

"We're at the end times," Jacob started to beam as if he was speaking to his congregation. "Why do you think the town is empty?" he questioned.

Before he could reply, Jacob answered his own question. "The rapture is *here*. I was sent to see the signs, and I *did*. I saw the bodies *all throughout the town*. I saw them *melted* in their houses; taken by the *hate* they stewed in. Even my dear Marion. Taken by her own hand, she knew the righteous hand of God was coming to judge her, and he would judge her unworthy of *His* grace. Now it's up to *me* to save us. This is the final sacrifice to save those who remain."

Anton could now only stare in panic, hate and confusion at the words Jacob had spoke.

"I have to offer you up. *Don't you see*? The demon's claws have gripped tight for a reason. You are embodying the evil which is killing the planet, so the evil must be punished. We will bring the world the salvation he will reward us with."

Placing his book onto the altar beside his brother, he did not notice that Anton had started to cry; the tears still blood red, fell down his face and landed on the stone which he lay.

The Sacrifice of Anton Stacey

Closing his eyes, Jacob began to speak a prayer, loud and bold. "At your command, O Lord, may the goodness and peace of our Lord Jesus Christ, our Redeemer, accept this sacrifice and banish the demons from us. In the unity of the Holy Spirit, God, forever and ever."

Still with a smile on his face, Jacob looked downward, but instead of seeing the tears in his brother's eyes, he only saw the same blue eyed glow that the dark form had, spilling from his sockets.

An unnoticed trickle of dark red blood, dripped from the corner of Jacob's mouth, into his beard hair, and down onto his shirt as he exclaimed under his breath. "Please God, steady my hand."

"Let me go. Please. I'm callin' in my chit," Anton softly begged to Jacob. He hoped those words would bring his brother out of his religious fervour. But it was futile; He could not hear Anton's real words. In his mind, his brother's was instead rasping vile insults at him in between screaming in tongues. His vision and hearing had been overrun with a false view of Anton, now a demon, tied to the altar , his real brother trapped inside.

"No!" Jacob shouted back as he turned toward something unseen that stood behind him. " You *promised* I could save him! He has gone, can't you see? The demon has won!"

"I'm your brother," were the next words Jacob did not hear Anton say. He could only hear two things; the snarls and obscenities that the demon tied to the altar spewed at him, and the commands of the voice which boomed behind him.

Jacob listened to his angel. His expression now dropped to understanding as he turned back to Anton, who still had the demon in his eyes. "He will bring you back to me." Jacob said in anguish. "But I *must* prove myself."

Anton's screams for mercy remained unheard. His pleas for his brother to stop only echoed to nothingness.

From beside his book on the Altar, Jacob grabbed a large knife he took from the church kitchen.

Neither of them had seen the rot that was now almost upon them, creeping at a slowed rate inch by inch. Anton started to cough as he felt his swelling pain return. Each cough more painful and strained than the one before.

"This my Lord is in your name. I offer up the dark one, as well as the blood of my kin," Jacob muttered weakly. His words steeled his hand to his mission. "*For you my Lord. For you my brother. For humanity.*"

He gripped the knife tighter.

He grimaced as blood trickled heavier from his mouth and fell down his front.

"*For love, I prove myself*," were the last words Anton heard before his brother plunged the knife three times into him; Three times, this razor-sharp knife cut through him with ease and swiftness; Once through his throat, and out the back of his neck. Once in the groin, the blade slicing through to his rectum on the other side. Once in his heart, the blade cut straight through his ribcage, and lodged into his spinal column.

Jacob was deaf to the short screams of agony his brother let out. He gasped as blood still dripped unknowingly from his mouth. Letting go of the knife lodged in his brother's chest, he turned his attention upward with a bloody smile.

The darkness outside the church was soon split in two by a light which slowly illuminated in the sky, coming toward the church fast. This light fell though the stained-glass window, casting multiple colors down onto the altar. It bathed the murdered remains of Anton in beautiful red, blue and green hues.

The Sacrifice of Anton Stacey

Jacob turned with glee to the invisible presence that he believed stood behind him. His eyes, now oozing blood, remained wide and joyful. "He's come," Jacob uttered gleefully under his breath. "Did I do good?"

He then turned back to admire his handiwork on the Altar. He smiled at the violent act he had forced upon Anton. It was *all* on behalf of his Lord. Jacob felt chosen. Jacob felt sanctified. Jacob felt blessed.

He slowly fell to his knees, as he raised his hands up in praise. "Hallelujah," he softly said. *"Hallelujah*!!!"

The light grew from outside in brightness as it came nearer. Jacob closed his eyes as he felt the invisible presence place one hand on his shoulder in comfort.

"I did the Lord's work. I'm his willing servant," Jacob smiled to himself, feeling a rising happiness unlike anything he had ever felt before.

"Praise him. Hallelu-!" his words were cut off as he coughed violently, stealing him away from this holy moment. A cough so vicious it brought forth a torrent of blood and gore from deep within his body, spewing out and all over Anton's corpse.

Within an instant, all of Jacob's flesh and bone liquefied and was ejected forcefully from every orifice. As these insides escaped, what was left of his body soon crumpled into an skin pile onto the stone floor.

With a renewed and aggressive speed, the rot crept forwards and crawled over the two brothers' remains. Consuming them with its blackened mold.

Somewhere in the night sky, the sound of helicopters cut through the silence of the town.

8
THE EPILOGUE OF FOLKSVILLE

A man dressed in military fatigues, with a rifle slung over his shoulder, looked through the metal fence which ran across the top of the mountain above Folksville. He glanced down over the ruins of this town. His thoughts rested on the millions of dead which had perished from the rot which overtook the world and now sat motionless far below him.

The once United States now stood proud and resilient as the United Remnants. From the Appalachians to the eastern sea board was all that remained of any kind of habitable earth. With no enemy to shoot, the world had been overcome with a terrible and unexplainable disease. Taking over the planet in a matter of days, it had only left a sliver of American coast line, housing any real population. For the last three years they had banded together. Created a society as best they could. Tried to live a normal life. But normal was now long behind them.

The remaining human race left had no idea what had happened to them. No idea what the rot was, or why it stopped its progression half way up this mountain. No idea why it didn't carry on over the rest of the country and kill them all; It wasn't the cold, as the freeze had long gone and the last few summers had been hotter than ever. This murderous mold had halted its journey at the Stacey cabin as if it was through with its purpose, as in 7 billion people were enough for it.

The soldier remembered that day, three weeks after the outbreak; the day he had arrived in Folksville. Dressed in full biohazard gear, he and his unit swept through the town, as they did many others, looking for fuel or anything else usable and not infected. They went from house to house searching, seeing the remains of those now dead, but found nothing of worth. Nothing really salvageable.

He had also been the one who was the first to sweep through the church. Within which he saw the two bodies on the altar, now covered in spores and growths from the rotting mold all over them.

He had no idea of who they were, nor who anyone in this town was. Neither he nor anybody else would ever know that Jacob Stacey believed that he did God's work. That he killed his brother, Anton, in order to save those who survived this apocalypse's wrath. Then again, if people *did* know their story, would they have believed that Jacob was right? That his God stopped this plague in its tracks? All because he slaughtered his brother?

This sacrifice of Anton Stacey could have been the defining act which started a new strand of religion. A new faith which could have infected the minds of those lucky souls who had survived. It could have spread through the United Remnants as fast as the rot infected the world, bringing a new way of thinking to a desperate band of survivors. There would always be forces that would want to silence those voices in most need of being heard, because if those voices spoke loud enough, miracles could happen.

But here, they did not.

Here this story would be forever unknown.

Anton Stacey had sacrificed a lot in his lifetime; his father, his home, his town, his life, all in exchange for a feeling of belonging which he did not get in Folksville. Jacob Stacey had sacrificed as well. He had sacrificed two things. Both being Anton. Jacob had sacrificed him once, when his misspoken words started a chain of events which resulted in the family breaking up. The other when he murdered his brother in cold blood.

Despite Jacob's holy beliefs, The sacrifice of Anton Stacey was in fact of no consequence to the world. It still turned no matter what Jacob had chosen to do. The diseased rot still took them away from their lives. No-one's God could, or did stop that from happening.

The soldier lit a cigarette as he walked along the fence which separated these two worlds; The world of death and the world of life. He walked up the path ahead of him, toward a makeshift military lookout which had been built on one of the lower peaks.

As the hill got steeper, this soldier began to sing to himself. A song that he wished he could hear again instead of only having a memory of it. There were no longer any radio stations to play it. No internet to stream it. He would only ever hear this song again in the echoes of his own mind.

I leave the cold mountains, as they leave me
    A life I must escape with glee
    I love you, brother, but you must see
    Goodbye is what must be
    Our time has flown
    Goodbye Appalachia
    Farewell my friend
    Goodbye Appalachia
    Our time now the end
    Goodbye Appalachia
    I'll maybe come back again
    Goodbye Appalachia